THE CHALLE
GROWING UP

A NOVEL

BY:
SAM CHOLERTON

Copyright Information.

This is a work of fiction. Names, characters, places, and incidents either are the product of the author's imagination or are used fictitiously. Any resemblance or appearance to actual persons, living or dead, events, or locales is entirely coincidental.

Copyright © 2022 Sam Cholerton

All rights reserved. No part of this book may be reproduced or used in any manner without the written permission of the copyright owner (Author) except for the use of quotations in a book review. For more information, email the Author:
SamMorley986@hotmail.com

I want to thank my family, friends, and my partner John for always having faith in me while I have been doing these stories.

I want to thank my editor who has helped me to do these stories.

Most of this story is about my life and how it was for me as a child and about me growing up.

CHAPTER 1

It was a nice Autumn Day on 8th November; it was Patrice's 16th birthday. She lived with her parents Charlotte and Andrew in Chilwell, and their house was like a mansion as it had 8 bedrooms and even a gaming room with their Parrot Winston.

Charlotte had brown short hair and blue eyes and was 40 years old and Andrew had a bald head and he had brown eyes, were planning something special for Patrice's birthday as they had something important to tell her. When Patrice woke up, she ran downstairs to the living room where her parents were sitting by Winstons' cage.

When she sat down, Charlotte said, "Happy birthday sweetheart how're you feeling now your 16?"

Patrice was jolly as she was classed as a young adult, "I am over the moon mum as it will not be long until I can leave school, as I hate being at school. As I am always a loner and I do not have any friends and when it is dinnertime, I am always wondering round the school grounds by myself and when other kids see me, they point and laugh at me because I am all alone."

Andrew spoke up and said, "Well darling we have a very nice surprise for you after school but first things first, do you want to open your present me and your mum brought you?"

For many years Patrice has always asked for a puppy, but she never got one as she wanted something to look after as she could not really look after a parent.

Patrice looked shocked as she did not expect anything special from her parents, but she was over the moon that her dad had said that "Oh you didn't have to get me anything special, but I appreciate it; yes, please I would love to open my special present from you guys."

Andrew handed Patrice a nice big basket covered up but when Patrice saw it, she did not look happy as she thought it was a basket of fruit and her parents know she hates fruit even though it is good for you.

Andrew said, "Don't worry it's not what you think it is as I can tell on your face you think it's a basket of fruit, if you take the cover off you will know what it is."

Patrice chucked the blanket off the basket and noticed that there was a clue inside, telling her where to find her surprise which read:

"**You will need to go into the garden to the shed and that is where you will find your surprise.**"

Patrice ran as quickly as she could to the shed and she found a puppy which was a Golden Retriever who was excited when she saw Patrice coming towards her as she was tied up with a bow around its chin with a note saying "Happy 16th Birthday sweetheart"

After she had her breakfast, she went back to her bedroom to carry on getting ready for school.

When she was ready, she was just about to walk out the door when her mum shouted, "Hang on a minute darling, there is just one more thing I have to tell you, you have to make sure that you come straight home from school and no going to the shop for sweets on the way home you understand?"

Patrice nodded her head then walked out the door to go and catch the school bus, but while she was waiting for the bus there was a group of girls who also go to the same school as her and totally ignored her, so she decided to wait in the door way of a flower shop until she saw the bus coming and she started to talk to the shop owners who were nice and friendly to her.

When the bus came, Patrice started to walk to the back of the bus when suddenly, Susie who was tall and skinny and looked like a bad ass women says to her "Excuse me but you know that you can't sit at the back of the bus as this is for the older children of the school you need to get back to where you're supposed to sit."

Patrice does as she's told, and she was shaking a lot as she didn't want to get beat up goes back down to where the kids in her year group sat, a couple came and sat next to her and they started doing things that they shouldn't do on the bus a girl called Angel said to Patrice, "Can you do me a favour please as you're too young to see this, can you turn around as you don't want to see this; and I don't want any peeping toms looking at me and me and my fella kissing and probs' other things."

After Angel said this all of the other kids on the bus started laughing at Patrice and started shouting and laughing, "WE HAVE A PEEPING TOM ON THE BUS."

Patrice started to cry and turned to look out of the window. Suddenly, a girl came and sat with her as there were no other seats left. "Hi, my name is Nicky am I okay to sit next to you please as there are no other seats that are free?"

Patrice replied while she was looking around the bus as she did not really want to sit with anyone, so she shrugged her shoulders "Hi my name is Patrice and I guess you can sit here if there are no other seats available."

After Nicky sat down, they started talking and Patrice found out that Nicky is having the same sort of problems as she is at school.

Patrice says to Nicky, "You fancy being mates as I am going through the same sort of thing as you and I am getting picked on all the time and I don't have any mates either."

When they arrived at school which had 3 floors for different lessons, Nicky hugged Patrice after they got off the bus and they headed to their lessons.

CHAPTER 2

After school, Patrice wanted to get back home quickly to see her puppy and she was still thinking of a name for her pup, and she had a horrible day at school as she was getting picked on by everyone as they were calling her names so she rushed to get to the bus when Nicky was walking past to get the bus back when she saw Patrice was having a bit of trouble, as she fell over, so she helped Patrice up onto her feet and walked down the hill with her to the bus.

When they both got on the bus, there was this girl in Patrice's class called Edith who always sat behind them Edith pushed Nicky out of the way and sat right next to Patrice, "Ha-ha, I heard you fell over and everyone saw your pink pants, no one likes a thick stupid person like you. You do not have any friends; which is funny, and you are funny looking as well, and I know where you live" she laughed maliciously.

After Edith said that to Patrice, Patrice stared out of the window and started to cry as Edith was picking on her all the way home. Which made her feel like a tramp as Edith was also throwing things at Patrice.

Patrice thought she would get off the bus a few stops before hers and walk the rest of the way home.

When she got off the bus, she ran as fast as she could to get home while she kept on looking behind her to see if Edith was following her.

When she opened her front door, and got inside, she slammed it shut and ran straight upstairs to her room and slammed her bedroom door as well.

Charlotte heard Patrice slamming her bedroom door, she got worried as that morning Patrice was so jolly and happy as it was her 16th birthday.

Charlotte knocked on Patrice's door, "Darling, can I come in please? I am worried about you as you were all happy and jolly this morning."

Patrice wiped her eyes and went downstairs with her mum to say hello to her grandparents. When she got into the living room, Patrice looked shocked as she only thought it was her grandparents but then she noticed that her mum tricked her in thinking it was just her grandparents as it was most of the family as well like her uncle and auntie who were her mother's sister and brother-in-law and Patrice's uncle was from Jamaica and he was shy at family events even though he had been married for 10 years.

When Patrice and Charlotte got into the living room, the whole family shouted, "HAPPY BIRTHDAY."

Patrice went to sit next to Paul, her granddad and gave him a big hug and Paul said, "Wow I cannot believe your 16 already where has the time gone? I have a little something for you; what your parents do not know about, I have hidden it in your coat pocket, when you ran upstairs. I did not want your parents knowing what I have given you as your grandma do not even know I have giving you something extra, so it's got to be our little secret."

Patrice went to get herself a drink and while she was heading towards the kitchen, she quickly went to have a look in her pocket and found an envelope that her granddad put in there. When she opened it, she found a nice little necklace which was like a pendent and it could hold a picture in there which belonged to her great-great grandmother when she was 16 years old and with it £50 as well.

Patrice could not believe what her granddad gave her, and she started to cry in the kitchen and Paul noticed that Patrice was crying. He went over to her, "I take it you liked your present, as I wanted to give you the necklace as your mum is allergic to silver and I wanted to give you a little something extra"

Patrice gave her granddad a big cuddle and said, "I love it thank you, can you put it on for me please. Do not worry; I will not wear it for school, just for special occasions in case it gets nicked or broken."

Paul and Patrice headed back into the living room and sat down before anyone wondered what was going on. Charlotte was just about to head into the kitchen to see why Patrice was crying again, Charlotte said, "Dad have you upset Patrice as I have only just calmed her down before we came downstairs?"

Paul replied, "Of course not darling, we have just been having a nice chat that's all."

Once everyone was sat down, Andrew went into the kitchen to fetch Patrice's birthday cake that he made, and Andrew shouted, "Can someone turn the lights off please and Patrice can you stand up for me?"

Patrice stood up but her legs were like jelly after the day's events and then family all started to sing happy birthday.

Andrew started to walk towards his daughter with the big cake that he made but just before he got to Patrice, he dropped the cake on the floor, and everyone started to laugh. Charlotte said, "Don't worry darling I have a spare cake in the kitchen that I picked up this morning as I thought we might need a spare one."

Andrew could not believe that Charlotte went behind his back and got another cake as this should have been his job to make sure Patrice had a good cake.

CHAPTER 3

The next morning after Patrice's 16th birthday party, Charlotte had to go and wake Patrice up as she overslept and had not left for school. When she got to her bed, she noticed that Patrice was not breathing. Charlotte quickly shouted to Andrew "You need to ring 999 quickly as Patrice is not breathing and she has gone blue and hurry! I tried to ring for an ambulance, but I could not as I kept on getting panicky to talk."

Andrew came running up the stairs with the phone against his ear and he told the operator everything she needed to know and the operator said to Andrew, "I know this is a stressing time for you all at the moment but please can you let your wife know that we have arranged for an ambulance to come to your home address straight away and can you stay on the line until it arrives, please sir."

While Andrew was on the phone, Charlotte kept on trying to wake Patrice up and she tried everything she could think of, like shaking Patrice to see if she was pretending so she did not have to go to school as Charlotte knew that Patrice hated school.

After 5 minutes of Andrew being on the phone, the ambulance turned up and Andrew let the operator know and then he put the phone down.

Andrew rushed downstairs and let the ambulance crew in and said, "It's my 16-year-old daughter, my wife went up to see her this morning as she is normally awake about 7.30am to get ready for school but when it got to 8am Patrice still hadn't woken up and that's when my wife found that she was still in bed and not moving or breathing."

The paramedic said, "Thank you for letting us in, do not worry we will try our best to help your daughter. Andrew had explained where Patrice's bedroom was, and they went straight up.

"Is she on any medications or anything?" Andrew shook his head while the paramedics went over to Patrice's bed and fitted breathing equipment onto her.

"It looks like we will have to take her down to Harbour General and get her booked in, but I am afraid there is only 1 person allowed in the back of the ambulance with us."

Charlotte looked at Andrew who nodded and followed them in his car. While Charlotte was sitting in the back of the ambulance with her daughter, Patrice kept on coming round then going again so they had to put the blue lights and the sirens on as this was an emergency. The traffic was bad as it was rush hour. When they arrived at Harbour General, they quickly took Patrice to ITU to do some tests and put her on a life support machine; Charlotte and Andrew sat in the waiting room until they were finally allowed in with her.

After they did a few tests to find out what was wrong with Patrice, a doctor came to see the family and to explain what they have found out. Doctor Margaret said, "Patrice has a very rare disorder called Guillain- Barre which means that her bodies' immune system attacks her nerves- weakness and tingling in the hands and feet are normally the first symptoms to appear."

Charlotte replied, "So what does that mean for Patrice then?"

Margaret replied, "That means that it often starts a few days or even weeks after Patrice has had an infection such as a stomach bug or the flu. Also, symptoms usually develop over hours or even days and tend to start in your feet or hands before spreading to other parts of your body. Sorry to say this, but we will have to keep Patrice in for a few days until she has stabilised."

Charlotte and Andrew looked shocked, as Patrice never mentioned anything about her having an infection, a stomach bug, or the flu to her parents.

Charlotte replied, "Yes, of course we understand that- we have just celebrated her 16th birthday as well. We will go home now then if that is okay, so you can carry on with the tests you have to do."

Andrew, however, replied, "Actually, Charlotte would you mind if I stayed with her, please, as she's my little girl and before you say that she's yours as well, I know that- but I would appreciate it if you wouldn't mind me staying, and if you want to, we can take it in turns to stay with her?"

Charlotte squeezed his hand, saying "Of course I understand and, yes, I would appreciate it if we could take it in turns, as I still have a job, but I also know that at this time my job is not really important as our daughter is more important, but I need to keep busy. It might not be so easy for me to get the time off; we are short staffed at the moment. Have you got everything you need like your phone and your phone charger?"

Andrew replied with some tears running down his face, "Oh shit, I forgot my charger, and I don't have my bank card on me, would you be able to go and pick them up for me please?"

Charlotte started to cry as she was getting so upset seeing her little girl like this and all tubes on her, "Yes of course, I need to keep in touch with you at all times, so I will go now and be back say in an hour or so, but I will let you know when I am on the way back."

CHAPTER 4

The next morning, before Charlotte went to work; she rang Andrew up: "Morning how is our little girl today? And more to the point how are you, did you sleep well?"

Andrew replied, "I could not sleep as I was so worried about her, I know it will not be easy, but we have to try and concentrate as much as we can. You need to keep busy; I will see you after work wont I?"

"Yes, you will see me after work and I will ring again while I am on dinner break as well, just to see if there are any updates. Also, think my parents are coming in as well today to see Patrice but they do not know what time yet. I will get them to ring you when they are on the way."

After Andrew got off the phone, he got ready to go down to the café to get something to eat and drink, when he noticed that it had been snowing outside, not much, but he was so thrilled to see it as he used to love the snow when Patrice was younger, when they would go into the garden and build a snowman together.

Later that day, Charlotte's parents turned up to see how Patrice was getting on,

Patrice's Grandad Paul and Patrice's grandma Gabbie came in to see how Patrice was doing Gabbie said, "Hi Andrew how are you? You look so tired did you get any sleep? Why don't you go and get some fresh air or something and me and Paul will sit with Patrice till you get back?"

Andrew nodded and he headed downstairs to get a hot drink and something to eat, then he went outside the main entrance for some fresh air.

After half an hour of Andrew being outside in the cold, trying to clear the over-heated stuffiness of the hospital from his brain, he just felt that he really needed to get back to his little girl, despite knowing that Gabbie was there.

Before he went back up, he decided to go into the gift shop to see if he could find something for his daughter, and he found a lovely white teddy that he decided to buy for her and place at the side of her bed, for when she came around.

When he got back upstairs, he found his mum Samantha was waiting for him to come back.

Samantha said, "Hi son, how are you keeping? Hope you are keeping your energy levels up and eating properly?"

Andrew looked shocked, as he did not expect his mum to be there since he knew she had a bad cold, "Hi mum I didn't expect you to come as you said you were full of cold and I didn't want you to get worse- where's George, hope he's, okay?"

Samantha went to give her son a hug, but Andrew stood back as he did not want to catch anything, in case he passed it to Patrice, "What a delightful surprise you have come to see how your granddaughter is. I am also sorry that I had to step back when you tried to give me a hug, but I cannot risk getting a cold while I am staying with Patrice- hope you understand?"

Samantha replied, "Of course darling, I understand, no need to be sorry. I just wish I could help and take it all away from you all, I love you son. George is busy today, but he wants to come tomorrow, if that is, okay?"

Andrew started to cry, "You okay mum, as you hardly say 'I love you' to me unless something is wrong with you? Okay I cannot wait to see George as not seen him for a while, and we get on so well, and he is taken Patrice on like his own granddaughter."

CHAPTER 5

After a few days, while Andrew was asleep, a nurse turned up to check in on Patrice and she gently woke Andrew up, "Morning Andrew, hope you're okay, we might have some good news for you and your wife today, but I won't tell you until your both here if that's okay?"

Andrew struggled to wake up, and while he was rubbing his eyes, the nurse brought him a cup of tea.

 "Thank you so much for the cup of tea, and what sort of news have you got to tell us, as Charlotte would want to know before she comes in as she hates bad news."

"No, it's very good news, now that she has had two plasmapheresis operations- complete changes of blood- we are thinking of taking Patrice off the life support machine today, to see if she can breathe by herself, she's been doing so well with the medicine we have been giving her through her tube, and we think she might be strong enough."

Andrew could not believe what he was hearing so he quickly got his phone out and rang Charlotte,

"Darling you're never going to believe this, they are thinking of taking Patrice off her life support machine as she's been doing so well with taking her medicine through her tube and also, they think she is strong enough to breath by herself now."

Charlotte started to cry, "Oh wow that's brilliant news, as soon as I come off the phone, I am going to tell my manager that I need to come to the hospital as we both need to be there for when Patrice wakes up, can you do me a favour please, as I will be too busy rushing to get the bus to the hospital. Could you ring my parents for me please darling, and did you want to ring your mum and George to let them know?"

Andrew replied, "Yes of course darling, I will order you a taxi so you can get here quicker I will get it to pick you up from outside work and hope your manager will be okay with you leaving during your shift, but then if you have explained to him, he should be all right? Love you loads darling."

As soon as Andrew got off the phone to Charlotte, he booked the taxi for her and then he sends a group text to Charlotte's parents and his mum saying, **"Hi everyone just to let you know that the nurse is** on about taking Patrice off her life support machine today if you all want to be here to see her when she wakes up because she is strong enough without it."

Within 5 minutes of him sending the message, everyone replied, saying that they were on their way.

After Andrew sent that message, Charlotte arrived within 15 minutes after the taxi picked her up and she ran straight up to the ward front desk and said, "Hello, I was told they were on about taking my daughter off the life support machine today and that my husband wanted to wait till I was here."

After Charlotte arrived and let the reception team know that she was there, she rushed over to Andrew at Patrice's' bedside, and gave him a hug and a kiss then went over to Patrice and gave her a kiss on the cheek and whispered in her ear, "Hi darling, mummy is here now, and I can't wait for you to wake up and speak to us."

As soon as Charlotte whispered into Patrice's ear, the head nurse turned up with another nurse and said, "Morning Charlotte, hope you're well - you got here quickly, I didn't expect you here for about

30 minutes or so but guess the traffic wasn't that bad."

Charlotte smiled at the nurses as she could not speak as she was so overwhelmed that Patrice was doing so well, and that they were taking her off the life support machine today.

Within 30 minutes of Charlotte arriving, the rest of the family turned up as well and they all sat by Patrice's bed side. The nurse came over and said, "I am afraid there is only a maximum of 2 people next to her bedside, but you're more than welcome to take it in turns."

Charlotte and Andrew nodded, and ushered everyone else out into the waiting area, where they peered through the door window while the equipment was disconnected and removed.

After the life support machinery was gone, Patrice's' parents sat next to the bedside, and waited patiently for her to come around. No- one dared to look anywhere else, as they all wanted to be next to her for when she woke up.

After an hour of them all waiting patiently, with the grandparents swapping in and out at regular intervals, Patrice opened her eyes and she looked dazed and confused as to why she was in hospital, as she did not know what had happened. All of her family was so relieved, as only the day before, things had seemed so touch and go.

Once Patrice had managed to focus her vision a bit, she said, "Where am I? What happened to me?"

Charlotte replied while she was crying happy tears, "You're in hospital as you had an unbelievably bad reaction to something like an infection you might have had but you did not realise? Or did you have a stomach bug or something you did not tell us about?"

Patrice replied, "I just had a runny nose all the time and was coughing but I didn't think much of it really, why, is that why I am in hospital?"

Charlotte started to cry so Andrew had to take over explaining things to Patrice, "Darling you have something called Guillain- Barre, which means that your bodies' immune system attacks your nerves, and you get a weakness and tingling in your hands and feet which are normally the first symptoms to appear?"

Patrice replied, "Now, I remember having some tingling in my hands and feet, but I just thought that was pins and needles, so I didn't say anything, as I didn't want you to think that I was being a baby or anything."

Charlotte and Andrew both said, "Darling we would never think your being a baby, what made you say that?"

After an hour of Patrice waking up, George turned up with a snowman for Patrice, as he knew how she loved the snow when she was younger, she used to beg him to go and make a snowman.

The head nurse said to George, "You do know the snowman might melt as it is hot in here, but feel free to put him in the sink next to Patrice's bed if you want to."

Everyone laughed as they thought it was funny that George brought a snowman into the hospital. He put the snowman in the sink so it did not make a mess as it melted, and so Patrice could enjoy looking at the snowman despite being unable to go out in the snow to play.

CHAPTER 6

The next day, some more family members came in to see Patrice and this time it was her auntie Angie who was her mum's sister and her husband Trevor, and also Patrice's great grandma, Michelle.

They all gave Patrice a big hug as they were all relieved that Patrice was doing well without her life support machine.

During the day while the family were visiting Patrice, Michelle asked "Are you comfy being in bed or did you want to sit on this comfy chair as I think some of your mum's work mates are coming in to see you as well later and think they are bringing you something to do."

Patrice replied, "Actually I have spent ages in bed, so yes please grandma can you help me into the chair as I still can't walk properly but they are doing some exercises with me to build my strength up as someone needs to hold me while I am walking in case I fall over."

While Michelle was helping Patrice into her chair, Charlotte turned up and said, "Grandma you shouldn't be helping to put Patrice into the chair as you're not strong enough and that should be the nurse's job to do that."

While Patrice was sitting in her chair and playing some games with the family, the nurse came over and said, "Hi sorry to bother you Patrice, while you are with family, but I just wanted to let you know that if you ever get bored and want to learn while you are in here then we have a classroom that you are more than welcome to go and use. There are other children like you who go in there so they do not get bored, and they can still carry-on learning while they are in here and you can also make some new friends as well."

Patrice looked at the nurse and replied, "I don't have many friends and it would be good for someone to talk to while I am in here as much as I love my family it would also be nice if I had someone my own age to talk to."

After an hour of her family visiting, it was time for Patrice to have some dinner, but Patrice could not eat like any normal person, she had a tube in her nose, and she had to be fed through the tube.

Charlotte fed her while the family were still there, but after an hour the family left as they had dinner plans, but they wanted to see Patrice before they went for left.

After Angie, Trevor and Michelle spent an hour with Patrice, they all said their goodbyes as they were going to meet Patrice's gran, Susan in Beeston as Susan had a hair appointment, so she could not be at the hospital that day to see Patrice. Sally said, "I have just had a text off your Gran and she said sorry she couldn't come in to see you today but she will come and see you another day with me and your great grandma and she also keeps praying for you to get better and stronger and also that she loves you dearly, and she's also full of cold and she didn't want to pass it on to you or your mum."

Patrice nodded and said, "That's okay I understand please tell Gran not to worry and that I love her dearly too."

Everyone gave Patrice a kiss and a cuddle but just before they left, Michelle said to Patrice, "Here is £20 for you to get something you want from the shop when you go downstairs or ask your mum or dad to save it for you but don't waste it and spend it wisely."

Patrice could not believe that her grandma gave her some money, so she gave her a big hug and said, "Thank you so much grandma."

After her grandma gave her the money, everyone left so that Patrice could have her dinner in peace, Andrew said, "Darling you are going to have some more visitors later today or tomorrow which will be grandma and her 2 sisters Betsy and Lola."

Patrice replied with a smile on her face, "I can't wait to see them as I have not seen grandma for a while and I love seeing her as she teaches me how to knit, and she makes the nicest meat and potato pie."

CHAPATER 7

The next day, Margaret came and did her rounds to make sure everyone was okay, when she got to where Patrice and Andrew were, she said, "Morning, hope you both slept well? Patrice, I was just talking to some other members of staff, and we were thinking if you wanted to do this, you see, we have a teacher who comes in once a week on a Thursday; if you wanted to go down and do some activities with the other, poorly children who are in the same boat as you? I know your legs will not be strong enough just yet, but we have a special wheelchair that we can take you down in, and you can also meet some new people. It will give your dad some time to either go home or for him to go and catch up on a few things."

Patrice replied, "Yes that would be nice; as it would be good to speak to some people my own age and who are going through the same sort of thing as I am. Plus, I agree it's not fair that my dad is always here when I know that he has stuff he could be catching up on... although I love my dad millions, but he has his own life to live as well."

Margaret smiled and replied, "Of course I will go and sort that out for you right away."

Once Margaret went to sort out everything for Patrice, she came back with a special sort of wheelchair to take her down to the classroom, "Here you go, Patrice, I can take you down to the classroom or your dad can, that's up to you?"

Patrice smiled and Andrew helped Margaret to get Patrice into the wheelchair "Would it be okay if my dad came down with us, so he knows where I am, in case he needs me for anything, or my mum needs to know where I am?"

Once Patrice was in the chair, Margaret and Andrew took her down to where the classroom was and Margaret introduced them to everyone, "This will be where you come when you either want some space or if you want to do some learning and this is your teacher, Bob, who is tall and skinny and he is so nice and friendly and also supports Forest and you can have a laugh with him."

Once Patrice was settled in, Andrew said "Are you going to be okay if I head out and do some things, I need to catch up on; I have my mobile with me if you need me to come and fetch you if you don't like it here; just give me a message and I will come straight back and fetch you."

Patrice smiled at her dad, "I will be okay I think, as it seems nice in here and they have computer consoles like an Xbox in here which I love and also loads of crafting stuff which I also love to do as I can make you and mum something, and I will phone or text you if I need you but don't think I will."

After Andrew gave Patrice a kiss and a hug he left Patrice to her own devices, then Bob comes over, "Hi Patrice like Margaret said my name is Bob and I will be your teacher every week. We are a friendly bunch in here; we have another lad starting as well today and he will be here in about an hour. I think you two will make friends straight away, what did you want to start off doing while you are here?"

Patrice looked around to see what she wanted to start with first, "Can I go and do some crafting please if you can take me over to the table as my legs are not strong enough to walk as that's why I am in this chair."

Once Patrice was sat at the crafting table, she started to get bits ready to make a picture for her parents, this young lad comes over to her and says, "Hi my name is Bruce, Bob suggested that we sit together as I have just come into hospital, and I don't know anyone here and he thought that we might be able to become friends."

Patrice smiled, "That would be nice, yes of course you can sit with me as I am just making a picture for my parents then we can go over to the game consoles if you want and play a game with each other."

Patrice and Bruce started to make some drawings and they were having a right laugh with each other. Andrew rang Patrice to check in, "Hi sweetheart how you doing? Are you still enjoying it in the classroom; I can come back and get you if you want and do not forget that your grandma is coming to see you today with her two sisters and they are coming about 1 so I will come and get you at 12 if that is okay with you then I can give you some dinner before they come."

Patrice smiled down the phone to her dad, "Oh yes I forgot that grandma was coming in today I can't wait to see her and her sisters and that's fine about you coming to fetch me at that time and yes I am having a fantastic time here and I have made a new friend already, his name is Bruce."

After Patrice got off the phone with her dad, her and Bruce go over to the Xbox and they play Street Fighter and every time they play Bruce beats Patrice but that is only because he is a pro at that game as he has got it at home, and he plays it all the time.

After an hour of Patrice being beat at the game, they had one more game before her dad came to pick her up and this time Patrice beat Bruce at the round they were on and Bruce could not believe that she beat him, "See you're a pro at this game as you just beat me at that round." Patrice looked shocked, "You let me win on that round as you felt sorry for me, I do not mind if you did as I am no good at this game. I better get off now as my dad will be here for me in a minute as my grandma and her 2 sisters are coming in to see me today and I cannot wait."

Once her dad arrived to pick her up and to take her back upstairs to give her some dinner and to get her ready to see her grandma, Patrice smiled at her dad, "Dad this is my new friend I have made today, and his name is Bruce. I have also done you and mum a picture that is just about dry for you to take with us,"

Andrew smiled at Bruce, "Nice to meet you Bruce, my name is Andrew hope to see you again soon, and please feel free to come and visit Patrice any time on ward H4."

After Andrew introduced himself to Bruce, he took Patrice back up to the ward and got her some dinner while she is sat in her chair before her grandma and her 2 sisters turned up to visit them.

After an hour of Patrice having some dinner, her grandma turned up with her sisters and Patrice had a massive smile on her face, "Hello grandma how are you keeping and how are you Betsy and Lola?"

Betsy and Lola replied, "We are good thank you but how are you doing Patrice hope you are feeling a bit better? Have you done anything nice this morning?"

Patrice smiled at them both and said, "I am getting there, thanks for asking and I have made a new friend this morning as I have been in a classroom today. I made a picture for my mum and dad then I played on the Xbox against this lad called Bruce and he beat me on a game until he let me win one round."

Betsy and Lola smiled and then her grandma put a jigsaw puzzle on the table that was in front of Patrice's chair, "I was thinking that we could all do this jigsaw together if you wanted to? I know you love jigsaws do not you, we used to do them all the time when you came to visit me at mine."

Patrice smiled at them and then they all started to do the jigsaw together, even Andrew helped as well.

After a while of them all doing the jigsaw puzzle, Patrice's mum turned up, "Hi everyone hope you are all doing well? How was your morning Patrice, hope you had an enjoyable time down at the classroom, as your dad told me you went down and that you met a new friend called Bruce and that he let you beat him on a level on a game called Street Fighter that was nice of him."

Patrice smiled at her mum, "I am okay thanks mum, look who has come to visit me which is nice of them, why don't you and dad go and spend some time with each other as since I have been in here, you have not seen much of each other have you? This will be a good chance for you both to have some quality time with each other as you have not spent much time at all since, I have been in here and it is not fair that you have not seen each other much. I will be okay with grandma and her sisters."

Charlotte looked at Andrew then she smiled at Patrice and they both headed down to the cafeteria to get something to eat and drink and to spend some time with each other because while Patrice has been in hospital, they have hardly spent any time with each other or even seen each other and Patrice knows that her parents like to spend some time with each other as they go on date nights each month.

Once Charlotte and Andrew left to go and spend some time with each other, Patrice, her grandma, Betsy, and Lola spent some time with each other and they were having such a laugh with each other and they all decided to start knitting as Patrice had started something ages ago with her grandma while she was visiting her, and she brought it with her so they could finish it off together.

After an hour of Patrice doing some knitting with her grandma, her parents came back up to check on how they were doing as they thought it would not be fair to leave Patrice with her grandma and her sisters.

Patrice looked shocked that her parents were only gone for an hour, "What are you guys doing back, I thought you would have gone to the pub for something to eat and spend more time with each other, you do not have to worry about me as I am fine. I do not mean to sound nasty either but please go and enjoy yourselves as I am 16 now and I will be ok by myself if grandma and co needed to go."

Scarlett who was Patrice's grandma replied, "Patrice is right you go and enjoy yourselves we will be ok for another hour with her because Lola's bus is not due for another hour anyway and I am enjoying seeing Patrice as I always look forward to seeing her."

Charlotte replied, "Only if you're all sure you will be ok with Patrice as I do worry about her as she's my little girl and if anything happened to her, I don't know what I will do."

CHAPTER 8

The next morning, after the busy day of visitors, Margaret- Patrice's' doctor came and did her rounds again to make sure that everyone was ok. "Morning Patrice and Andrew how you both slept ok, do you want some good news this morning, I have been in a meeting with my manager this morning and we have decided that for 1 day a week if you wanted to Patrice, your parents or even a family member can take you out for the day as it will save you looking at the same 4 walls all the time wont it and you can go and see your family members who haven't been able to come and see you while you have been in here."

Patrice started to cry, "That would be great thank you so much, dad did you hear that I could go out 1 day a week if I wanted to."

Andrew replied, "Wow that's great news, I will let my wife know straight away and I can take Patrice places like McDonalds and place like that."

Once Andrew got on the phone to let Charlotte know, she started to cry down the phone, "Wow that's great as I know some of my work colleagues would love to see Patrice and I can bring her to work 1 day as well."

Once Andrew got off the phone Patrice said, "When can I start to go out, as I was hoping to see Bruce today and I was wondering if I could go and have a game with him on the Xbox to see if I could beat him again but without him letting me?"

Margaret replied, "That's up to you when you want to go out for the day, but before you go you will need to let one of us know so we can get things ready for you, that's fine if you want to see Bruce today as I can go and find another doctor to take you down to see if he wants a game with you on the Xbox if you can just hang on a minute, please then I will come and let you know."

Patrice nodded then Margaret went to check on Bruce to see if he wanted to have a game with Patrice and to see if he was busy with having any visitors or anything.

After an hour of Margaret going to check to see if Bruce was free, she comes back to Patrice "You're in luck Bruce is free for a few hours and he said he will beat you at the game again and, he said bring it on lol. So, I will just go and find a chair for you then I can take you down if you want."

Patrice smiled and laughed, "That will be brill thanks, I will just get dressed then I will be ready to beat his sorry little ass lol."

Margaret and Andrew both laughed their heads of, and Margaret went in search for a chair to take Patrice down to the games room.

After about 30 minutes of Margaret searching for a chair for Patrice, she comes back with one and both Andrew and Margaret help Patrice into the chair then the nurse took her down to the gaming room to meet up with Bruce.

When Patrice got downstairs, Bruce was already there waiting for her, and he already had a few rounds of Street Fighter before Patrice arrived. "Morning Patrice how are how feeling today you ready for me to wipe your back side?"

Patrice replied, "I am ok thanks just a bit tired this morning, and I hope you're ready for me to beat your back side on this game."

Margaret left the children playing Street Fighter and went back to do her rounds, when she got back up to the ward, Charlotte had just arrived, "Morning Margaret how was Patrice this morning, for some reason I cannot find my husband anywhere, but it is good news that we can take Patrice out once a week, so she gets some fresh air.

After 5 minutes of Charlotte being on the ward Andrew turns up, "Morning darling you, ok? I did not expect you to come today as thought you had work?"

Charlotte looked shocked as she thought she told Andrew that she had booked the rest of the week off so she can take over from Andrew and stay at the hospital, "I am sure I told you that I have booked the rest of the week off so I can stay with Patrice and you can go home and get some proper sleep, as bet you're not sleeping well as you're in the hospital with all the noise and everything?"

Andrew checked his phone again at the texts that Charlotte had sent him, "Oh yes sorry you did tell me that, I am half asleep as I am not sleeping very well in here, and I can't wait to be in our bed tonight."

Margaret replied, "I have just dropped Patrice off in the gaming room for a bit, so if both want to go and get some breakfast somewhere as if you do not fancy the café then there is a Weatherspoon's across the road if you want to go their called "Dreamers" and spend some time with each other this is probably the best time for you to do this while she is with Bruce, but I can always get her to text or ring you when she has finished?"

Charlotte and Andrew looked at each other, "That sounds like a great plan, I will ring Patrice and let her know we are going out for a bit and for her to ring or text us when she wants picking up or if she wants anything fetching."

Once Andrew got off the phone with Patrice both Andrew and Charlotte headed off to the pub to get something to eat and to spend some time with each other while Patrice is busy with Bruce.

Once they both arrived at "Dreamers" Charlotte went to go and get a table while Andrew went to the bar and orders the drinks, but while he was at the bar a lad goes over to him and says, "Sorry to bother you, but is your name Andrew Umar? And did you go to Wheelage School?"

Andrew looked at this bloke and replied, "Yes to both questions but sorry to sound rude but do I know you as you look familiar, but I can't picture who you are?"

The lad replied, "It's me Scott Bandmill we were in the same class with each other I might have changed since you last saw me though how you doing and are you married yet?"

Andrew looked puzzled as he could not remember anyone called Scott in his class, "Oh sorry I still cannot remember you at all but then again, I cannot remember everyone from back in the day. But how you doing these days and yes, I am married now, and I have a 16-year-old daughter my wife is over there waiting for me to bring the drinks to her. Also, she was my childhood sweetheart as we went to the same school as each other can you remember anyone called Charlotte?"

Scott replied, "Yes I can remember Charlotte I had a massive crush on her wasn't her surname Rockford?"

Charlotte was getting fed up of waiting at the table for the drinks as she was getting worried in case Patrice needed them back, "Darling do not mean to sound rude if you are talking, but I am getting hungry and I do not want to be out long in case Patrice needs us.

After Charlotte spoke to Andrew, she looked shocked as she noticed a blast from the past, "Oh my goodness Scott, Bandmill- what a blast from the past- how you doing? You have not changed1 bit since we were younger, and we lived on the same street as each other."

Scott looked at Charlotte, "Wow you look even more beautiful than I can remember, oh so you are the lucky lady who is married to this fine gentleman then? Wow Andrew you have a stunner here mate well done"

Andrew looked at Scoot with an angry face as he thought that Scott was trying to chat up his misses, "It was nice catching up with you mate but we are both starving and we have things to do, but it was nice chatting to you, but we must get on now."

Once Andrew grabbed the drinks, Charlotte and Andrew go back to the table and they ordered a full English breakfast on the app so he did not have to go back to the bar and bump into Scott again as he remembers why he could not remember him and that was because he was so full of himself.

Once the food had arrived, Andrew's phone start to ring and it was Patrice, "Hi dad how's you and mum? You anywhere nice? I was just wondering when you are both coming back but there is no need to hurry back. It is just that I am bored now, and I was hoping we could all go and get some fresh air?"

Andrew looked at Charlotte, "We have just got something to eat sweetheart, is everything ok, thought you was having fun with Bruce? We will come back once we have had something to eat if that is, ok?"

After they had finished their full English brunch, they headed straight back to the hospital and went to where Patrice was with Bruce in the gaming area of the classroom.

Charlotte went over to Patrice, "Is everything ok darling, as you look a bit weak and a bit pale, I don't recommend that we go in the fresh air today while you look like this as we don't want anything to happen to you."

CHAPTER 9

The next morning, Margaret came and did some extra tests on Patrice, because of how she had looked the day before, and because Charlotte had asked the nurse to check on her, as she was worried.

When Margaret had finished, she came back over to where Andrew and Charlotte were sitting.

"I have done loads of tests on Patrice, and I cannot find anything wrong with her, but in my opinion, I think she is simply doing too much, but it is good in one way as that means she wants to try and get back to normal."

Having said that, she turned to Patrice and said "Patrice, I know you might be bored in here, and not being able to walk as well as you did before you were brought in, so if its ok with you, I have asked a physiotherapist to come and do some exercises with you so we can get your legs stronger."

Patrice smiled, "That's a great idea, as I would love to be able to walk again, as it's not fair that I have to wait for people to come and take me places that I want to get to, so would that be ok if you can organise that for me, please?"

Margaret smiled back, "Yes off course I will do that for you, I will go and sort that out for you, and then I will come and let you know the plan."

Charlotte and Andrew looked at each other then back at Patrice, "Oh darling I am so proud of you wanting to try and walk, that's the best news I have heard for a long time, and we have every faith in you being able to walk again."

After quite a while of Margaret sitting on the phone at the desk to try and arrange an appointment so that Patrice can start to get her legs stronger, she came back with some good news, "I have spoken to the physiotherapist for you, and she said she can come and see you tomorrow afternoon. They cannot give us a time just yet, as they have other patients to see as well and they can normally run over time, but when I know a time, I will come and let you know if that is, ok? But if you want to try and do some steps while your parents are here, you can do."

Patrice looked at her dad with a smirk on her face, "Dad do you feel strong enough to try and help me with doing some steps now please- if not that's ok, I can wait till tomorrow till the physiotherapist can help me?"

Andrew looked at Charlotte then at Margaret with a puzzled look on his face, "Would that be ok if I tried to help her to do some steps now as surely that's a good sign that she wants to try and walk?"

Margaret looked at them all then she checked the time on her watch, "Yes that's fine as I have a spare half an hour until I have to go for my lunch, as I recommend that I am here in case Patrice feels wobbly or anything, so I can keep an eye out as well, but I will just have to go and fetch a walker and a hoist, in case Patrice feels wobbly."

Everyone nodded at Margaret then she went in search for the equipment that she needed in case anything happens while Patrice was practising walking again.

Charlotte could not believe that Patrice wanted to practise some steps with her dad, "Oh Patrice, I will have to let your grandparents know that you're going to try and walk, they will want to see this- if that's ok with you darling, they all want to be in the loop?"

Patrice smiled at her mum and nodded, then Charlotte got straight on her phone, and she sent a group text to everyone, "**Just to let you all know that Patrice is going to try and do some steps with her dad today and the nurse will be with us in case anything happens, but I do not think it will. If you want to all pop down in an hour or so then I can let you all know how she got on or if you want to come now, I can ask Margaret to wait till you are all here to see how wonderful she will be?**"

After she sent the text to everyone, she got replies in short order, saying that they were coming straight away.

Charlotte went up to the front desk to find Margaret "Excuse me Margaret, would you mind if we hang on for an hour or so, as my family want to see her do some steps if that's ok with you- they are so worried about her, and they want to see her walking as they thought she wouldn't be able to again?"

Margaret replied with a smile on her face, "I don't see why not, I will have to come back after my dinner hour though if you don't mind waiting a bit longer?"

Charlotte could not believe that the family would be able to watch Patrice doing some steps; she smiled at Margaret, "That would be wonderful, thank you so much; I will go and let my husband and Patrice know. Will it be ok if we take Patrice outside the main entrance so she can get some fresh air and to have a look around the gift shop please?"

Margaret looked at Charlotte and gave her a nod and a smile, then Charlotte went back to Andrew and Patrice and gave them the good news, "You will never guess what Margaret has said, she has said that it would be ok for everyone to see you walk darling, and also we can take you to the gift shop and for you to go and get some air first if you want to?"

Patrice was so over the moon that she could finally go and get some fresh air and have a look around the gift shop. Andrew and Margaret helped to get Patrice into her chair so she could go outside for a bit, and although it was against hospital rules, Margaret gave Patrice £5 to go and treat herself. She was so pleased with how far she had come.

Patrice gave her a massive hug, "Thank you so much, that means so much to me, but don't worry as I know you are not allowed to give money out to patients, I won't say anything and just hope you don't get into any trouble, as I don't want you to get the sack or anything?"

Margaret smiled at her while Patrice and her parents went downstairs on the little outdoor adventure.

After half an hour outside, Charlotte said, "I think its best if we go back upstairs now, as the family will be here soon, and Margaret will be off her lunch as well, then you can practice walking with your dad and show everyone how well you are doing! We have every faith in you darling."

Patrice looked at her parents, "I can't wait to take a few steps as I don't like relying on other people to take me places in my chair, and it's not fair on all of you."

They all headed back up to the ward and found that everyone was already there waiting to see Patrice take her few steps.

Charlotte said, "How did you lot get up here? We have been just outside for half an hour, and never saw you come in or even arrive."

Scarlett replied, "We all met up in Beeston, then we came on the tram as it was horrible trying to park last time, and to be honest it was Gabbie's idea to get the tram, and for us all to meet up in Beeston and have some lunch together."

Samantha then beamed a wide smile at Andrew, saying, "Hey darling, how are you doing, are you getting much sleep at all? Bet you are not keeping your strength up on hospital food, so I have brought you something decent to eat and drink."

Andrew looked and smiled at his mum, "Mother, you do know that I am a big boy now and that I can look after myself? I do know I am still your little lad, so I do appreciate it."

After everyone said their hellos to each other, Margaret came over with the hoist and a walking support for Patrice to hold onto in case she needed to sit down quickly.

Charlotte could not help but show a bit of shock on her face, as she was not sure how Patrice would manage taking a few steps with a little bit of help from just her dad.

Once Margaret had the equipment in place, Patrice said, "Will it be ok to try and take a few steps by myself- but I will need help getting up from this chair if my dad can help me with that instead please?"

Margaret replied with a smile on her face, "Yes, of course you can, you can do anything you want to do if you put your mind at it."

Andrew went over to where Patrice was sitting in her chair and both Andrew and Margaret helped to get Patrice up on her feet, while she herself was holding onto the frame in front of her; then Andrew went to the other side of the room, waiting for her to get to him.

Once Patrice was standing up, Margaret said, "Don't forget little steps to start with, as we don't want to push you too hard on your first go."

Patrice smiled at Margaret and then started to put one foot in front of the other, managing to do about ten steps before deciding she had to give up, as she was getting so wobbly and feeling as if she her legs were going to give way. Andrew said, "Come on sweetheart, you can do this, can you try and do about another 10 steps for us please then you will have reached me- but if you can't, don't worry, we can try it again another day."

Patrice was so determined to get to where her dad was, and that she did not want to let her family down, she gritted her teeth and made it all the way to his outstretched arms.

Margaret quickly grabbed the chair, so she could put it behind Patrice before she collapsed; she could see her legs were going like jelly by this point, and expertly manged to get her into the chair before she fell.

Everyone was so pleased that Patrice was so determined to reach her dad with her unsteady little steps. There was a burst of applause and congratulation, along with quite a few relieved expressions.

Once Margaret managed to get Patrice back into bed, she took the chair back to the stock room for use another time.

All the family members who were there could see that Patrice looked worn out by her efforts and agreed that she should get some sleep and they should come back the next day to see how she was.

Patrice nodded and smiled weakly, and said, "That would be brilliant, thank you, as I am so worn out now, and I can do with some sleep- but I don't want to be rude or anything as you have all come to see me and I am so grateful that you were here to see me take some steps."

Everyone left Patrice to get some rest and her parents said, "Honey, we will come back and see you in the morning if you don't mind, as we both need a good night's sleep tonight and the bed in here is not comfy to sleep on."

CHAPTER 10

The next morning, Patrice's parents came to visit her to see how she was getting on after the eventful day she had the day before. Charlotte suggested, "Darling, how do you fancy going out today, we can go to a pub or something if you fancy it, as my work mates have been asking about you and they all want to see you?"

Patrice smiled at her parents, "That would be lovely; I would really like that, as it would be good to get out of the hospital for a bit as I am sick of seeing the same four walls all the time."

Andrew went to find a nurse to check if that would be ok to take her daughter out for a bit so they can all spend some time with each other. When he got to the front desk there was a man on duty. "Excuse me, I was looking for someone who might be able to help me please, as me and my wife want to take our daughter out for the day, and we thought we better check to see if that's ok as I don't know where the wheelchairs are kept."

The receptionist looked up at Andrew, as he was just inputting some data on to his computer, "I can sort that out for you sir, is it for Patrice? As I remember Doctor Margaret saying something about either you or your wife asking for a wheelchair for her so you can take her out. I will go and find one for you and bring it straight over for you."

Andrew nodded and went straight back to where his daughter and wife were sitting, "The receptionist is going to look for a wheelchair for us as he said that's ok for us to take Patrice out for the day."

After five minutes or so, he came over to where they were all sitting, "Here you go, I have also had a word with the nurse who is looking after Patrice and she has asked me to ask you if you can make sure she is back for tea please, as she wants to try and take the tube out of her nose so we can try your daughter on solid foods if that would be ok with both of you?"

They could not believe what they had just heard, "That would be great, and yes we will make sure she's back for teatime." They had been praying for this to happen for a long time, as that would be an excessively big step forward.

Both Charlotte and Andrew lifted Patrice carefully and placed her in the wheelchair ready to go out for the day. Andrew said to Charlotte, "Darling I will go and fetch the car round and meet you at the front entrance, so Patrice doesn't have to go far to get into the car."

Both Charlotte and Patrice said goodbye to the nurses, and they headed for the corridor towards the lifts; on the way out of the ward, though, Margaret approached them and said "Hi, sorry to be a pain, but I will need to come out with you if you don't mind, so I can help you take Patrice to the car- the car park attendants don't like people sitting there for a long time just in case an ambulance needs to park up or if we have an emergency, It's also practical that I am there in case anything happens while you're putting her into the car, as it saves you putting your backs out or anything like that."

Charlotte nodded and they all went down in the lift to get to the main entrance, but they had to wait 5 minutes until Andrew managed to bring the car round, since there was a queue trying to get out of the car park.

Once Patrice was in the car and had her seat belt on, they all thanked Margaret for helping to bring her down for them to take her out for the day.

Once they managed to pull out onto the main road away from the hospital, they started to drive a route unknown to Patrice, as Charlotte and Andrew wanted to surprise her before they took her to see Charlotte's work mates.

Patrice asked "Where are we going, I thought we were going to Beeston to see mum's work mates? Isn't this the wrong way?"

Andrew replied, "Don't worry sweetheart, we are still going to your mum's work, but we want to take you someplace first and it's a surprise, so please no more questions."

Patrice pretended to zip her lips with her finger as she did not want to upset her parents by asking any more questions about where they were going.

After an hour of driving, Charlotte turned around to face Patrice and said "Darling, can you put this blindfold on for us please, as this is a surprise, and we don't want you to know where we are just yet."

Patrice nodded and did as she was told but could feel that they had started driving up a hill.

Once the engine stopped, Andrew got out first, got the wheelchair out, opened Patrice's' door, and put the chair next to Patrice so she could slide onto it, with Charlotte helping her since she was still blindfolded, and she did not know where the chair was or where she was going.

Once Patrice was in the chair, Charlotte took off Patrice's blindfold with a flourish and said, "Can you guess where we are darling? As you love this place and we promised that we would bring you here for a day before you got poorly."

Patrice looked around and noticed that some of her mum's work mates were also here waiting for them to arrive, "I cannot believe it! We have actually come to Greenland Festival; I have always wanted to come to this one and every year you have said that you could not afford to take me. Thanks, you two, I really appreciate it."

Both Charlotte and Andrew had big smiles on their faces. Andrew said, "That's not the only thing that is a surprise, if you look to your right, you might see some people that you will recognise."

Patrice quickly looked to her right and she noticed some of her mum's friends from work who came to see her, "Oh wow, your friends are here as well mum- that's a surprise, however, did they manage to get time off work to come to this festival?"

Patrice waved to them all, and they started to walk over to join them in watching the performers singing and dancing.

Everyone gave Patrice a huge hug, and Lauren, who had short red hair and a glamour model build and was her mum's best friend said, "It's nice to see you out for a bit, Patrice, hope you're having fun, and hope this was a huge surprise for you seeing us all here?"

Patrice smiled at them all as she was so glad that they had come along and surprised her, "Yes this was a brilliant surprise to see you all- did your manager let you all come out to this festival, as I bet virtually everyone from my mum's department is here?"

Another one of her mum's friends, Yolanda from Pakistan answered "Yes, everyone from your mum's department is here, including her boss,

Peter. I do not know if you have met him, but he is dead tall, and got huge biceps!"

Patrice loved men with big biceps, so she tried to spot where Peter was, but he was nowhere to be seen.

After about five minutes of Patrice scanning the crowd for Peter, she nearly jumped out of her skin, because Peter crept up behind her and made her jump, much to everyone's amusement...

A famous singer came on stage with their group, met with a roar by the audience. It was Patrice's favourite band "The Successors." Patrice could not believe this, and she looked up at her parents, "Did you two know they were going to be here today, as you know I love this band- they tell a story that one of the band members was picked on at school, so he decided to do a song about that."

Charlotte and Andrew looked at Patrice and grinned "Of course we did darling, why did you think we brought you here today?"

Without telling her parents what she wanted to try, so held onto the handlebars of her chair and stood up by herself just to see if she could do it, as she fancied a bit of a boogie, as they had opened their set with her favourite song "Life Can Be Hard."

Once Charlotte stopped talking to her manager, she looked around and saw that Patrice was standing up by herself and swaying to the music... Charlotte poked Andrew and said, while she was crying happy tears, "Darling look at our daughter, she is standing up by herself, and I can't believe that she is so brave- just wait until I tell Margaret."

Andrew quickly got near his daughter in case her legs went weak, and she fell over, but to everyone's relief, Patrice managed to stand up for the entire song, bopping and singing with a big fat grin on her face.

After the song, the lead singer of the band, Oscar, spoke with his oh-so-sexy voice into the microphone, "We have a special guest here with us today, she has not been very well and she has been in hospital with a rare condition, and I know that she loves our band, so I just want to invite Patrice Umar onto the stage, but only if she can manage it, as we have some special things to give to her- and we would also love to invite her to one of our concerts in Vegas as well when she is better!"

One of the bouncers had a portable ramp that could help Patrice get up on stage, after her dad had wheeled her down to the front so she could meet the band.

One of the other bouncers introduced himself as Steve "Hi Patrice, hope you are doing, okay? I am medically trained, so can help people in your situation who are just starting to walk again after they ended up in hospital in a coma. So, I can help you to climb the stairs to get up on stage, if you think you can make it? If your dad wants to stay at the bottom of the stairs and wait for you?"

Patrice looked at her father and he nodded his head, then Steve took Patrice up on stage and she enjoyed sitting up there, and she even sang one of their songs with them, called "Friendship."

After they sang the song at the end of their set, and it was time for a different group to go on stage, Steven helped Patrice down the stairs and into her chair, where she had a picture taken with the whole group. Oscar gave Patrice some gig tickets for her and the family to go to Las Vegas next year, and to stay in a posh hotel which was all paid for and all-inclusive besides.

Andrew said to Patrice, "I think it's time for me and your mum to take you back to hospital now darling, as we have been out for most of the day now, and it's getting near to teatime, and they will be expecting you back soon."

Patrice looked at her dad with a big fat smile, "Do we have to go now? As I am having the best day ever, as I got to meet my favourite band, got a signed t-shirt, and got my picture taken with them!"

Andrew gave a sorry shake of his head as they started to leave the staging area. Steven ran up to them and said, "Sorry to disturb you folks again, but the band forgot to give you this teddy, which has been signed by all of them, and they said that they will come and visit you again in hospital, before they carry on with their tour."

Patrice started to cry as she was so happy, "Oh, Wow! Okay, Dad, let's go back, as to be honest I am getting a bit tired and hungry now, but this really has been the best day ever - thank you so much dad."

CHAPTER 11

A few months had passed now, and Patrice was back at home with her family after being in hospital. Charlotte said, "Darling since you have not long come out of hospital, I want to keep you home for a bit longer, so I can keep an eye on you - just until your legs are a bit stronger, really, as I have noticed that you're still a bit wobbly."

Patrice looked at her mum with a smile on her face, "That's great, mum because to be honest, I know I will still get picked on, and I don't want to get picked on for not walking properly as well; on top of getting picked on for no reason at school."

Charlotte started to cry and left the room as she did not want her daughter to see her crying, as what Patrice just told her made her so upset. After five minutes gathering herself in another room, she re-joined Patrice, took a deep breath, and explained "Darling, I cannot keep you off for much longer though, as I have just had a letter from your head teacher saying you need to go back soon, and I can only keep you off for another two weeks, then you just have to go back to school. I can have a word with them, though, to see if they can do something to help you. Is that a deal?"

Patrice nodded and gave her mum a smile, then went up to her room to play on her favourite Disney computer game.

After an hour of Patrice being on the computer, Andrew shouted up the stairs "Pat, it's time for dinner now, can you come down and sit with us, please?"

When Patrice got downstairs, she went into the kitchen and sat down with her dad, while Charlotte dished up one of Patrice's favourite dinners- sausage casserole.

After a thoroughly enjoyable dinner, Patrice asked, "Can we do some more exercises on my legs please, so I can get them a bit stronger, so I don't have to rely on you guys to take me anywhere? Now we are home, I want to go and play outside when I want, and take Shaky for little walks?" Shaky was her birthday pup, who was growing fast.

Her parents looked at each other with concern, puzzled that Patrice wanted to do some exercises so that she could go into the garden: she normally hated playing outside. They were so glad, though, that she wanted to start to take Shaky out for walks, since after coming back home, she hadn't really been that interested in Shaky at all. The dog was still getting used to having this third human around, too.

Andrew replied, "Yes of course we can, Pat, and if you want, we can all take Shaky out for a nice little walk, as she has missed out on getting to know you while you have been in hospital. Only if you want to go, of course, and only after we have had some pudding - your mum has made trifle for us all, as that's your favourite."

After they all had their delicious pudding, Patrice called Shaky over to put her lead on her to take her out for a nice walk around the block; that would also help with strengthening Patrice's legs at the same time.

They all got ready to go but Charlotte had to help get Patrice's shoes and socks on for her, otherwise Patrice would be their ages: she still struggled with bending her legs enough to put her shoes and socks on.

When they eventually got out of the house, they decided to go to the local park to do a bit of obedience training with Shaky, since they hadn't had time to do much with her while they were busy with visiting their daughter in hospital on top of everything else.

Once they arrived at the park, they let Shaky off the lead for a bit, to see how she got on. It was an enclosed space on the field, and usually not many people were around at that time of day.

Patrice sat down on the bench for a few minutes, so she could get her breath back after the walk from home. She watched her parents do some sit, stay, and come, training with Shaky. Patrice didn't know much about how to train a dog, as she had never had one before, but her parents were experts since both had dogs when they were growing up.

After five minutes of rest, she took a slow walk over to where her parents were. "Can I try and do a bit of training with Shaky, please? I would love to have a go, as she is my dog at the end of the day, isn't she? You both bought her for me, didn't you?"

Charlotte replied with a huge smile on her face, "Of course you can, Pat and yes, she is your dog, but we thought we would train her up for you, as she is still a bit jumpy, and we didn't want her to knock you over- you're still not very steady on your legs yet. But yes, you can call her to come back to you if you want, when your dad throws her the ball."

After Andrew threw the ball for Shaky, Patrice shouts, "Shaky go, and fetch the ball for me please!" Andrew had a little smile at how polite Patrice was being with the dog.

Instead of her bringing the ball back to Patrice, she took it straight to Andrew instead; Patrice started to cry. "Why won't she bring the ball back to me when I told her to go and fetch it?"

Andrew's face fell, as he hated seeing his daughter so upset, "It's okay, darling, you just must give Shaky a bit more time to get used to your voice – you shouldn't forget you were in hospital for a long time, she did not have much time to get used to your voice. We can keep trying though don't worry. We can come back again tomorrow and the next day until she gets used to you telling her what to do. Next time, keep the command nice and simple, just one word, FETCH!" Patrice tried again, doing as she was told, but Shaky still got a bit confused, bringing the ball back to Andrew.

Charlotte put Shaky back on her lead, as she could tell her daughter was upset and it tore at her heart to see it. "Don't worry sweetheart, she will get used to your voice like your dad said. Why don't you go and play on the park swings and things for a bit, then we can go home and watch a movie of your choice?"

Patrice nodded but when she was on the way over to the park equipment, she saw Susie, one of the kids who went to her school, taking her little sister onto the park. Susie shouted, "Oh, hi Patrice, how are you? I heard what happened, how are you feeling now?" Susie had a fake smile, plastered to her face as if all she wanted was playground gossip.

Patrice looked back at her parents, as they knew this was one of the kids who were picking on her while she was at school. Her dad called over "It's time to go home now, darling, as its Shakey's dinner time."

Patrice turned to her dad with a smile on her face, "Okay dad, coming!"

On the way home, Patrice looked up at her dad, "Thanks dad, as I was so scared, as she is one of the bullies at our school. She's a cow who always bullies people she doesn't like, and I think she was just being nice as she saw I was with you two."

Andrew smiled at his daughter as they made their way home at an easy stroll, with Shaky pulling on the lead enthusiastically, since another word she had learned was 'dinner.' Charlotte said, "Why don't you nip into this video shop darling, and choose a movie for us to watch, and get some popcorn and some sweets for us as well?" This, of course, was in the days before satellite TV and films on demand.

Patrice smiled and headed into the shop to have a look around, but there were loads of DVDS to pick from, and she couldn't decide on just one, so she picked about four DVDS for them to watch, and then headed over to the till with some munchies to eat during the film.

When she got to the till, Andrew nipped into the store with his membership card at the ready, and prepared to pay for them all, but when he noticed what she had picked, he didn't look happy- one of them was an 18. He kept his thoughts to himself for the meantime, though, not wanting to upset Patrice again.

Once they got home, Patrice fed Shaky while Andrew made them all a nice cup of tea, with some chocolate biscuits on the side.

After they all sat down and watched "Family Fortunes" Patrice yawned and stretched. "Boy, I feel dead weak now. I think I will go and have a lie down on my bed for an hour or so, if you don't mind?"

Her parents both smiled at her, as she headed straight up the stairs for her lie down.

After an hour of Patrice snoozing peacefully, she woke up as she felt something cold and wet on her face, "Oh hi, Shaky, you frightened me then, that's a nice wakeup call!"

When Patrice woke up properly, she was pleasantly surprised that there was a steaming cup of tea next to her on her bedside table, silently sneaked in by Charlotte. When she got downstairs after finishing her very welcome cup of tea, she went to her parents in the kitchen and said, "Thanks for the cup of tea, whoever made it, and thanks for the lovely wakeup call as well."

Charlotte laughed and said, "You're very welcome sweetheart, we thought we would let Shaky wake you up for a change, as you looked so peaceful, and neither me nor your dad had the heart to disturb you!"

Patrice also laughed and said, "I wouldn't have minded, but Shaky was a nice surprise!"

Everyone headed into the living room for some family time alone, without any guests or interruptions; both Charlotte and Andrew turned their mobiles off, and they even unplugged the land line for a few hours while they watched a film in perfect peace.

Since Patrice had picked several DVD'S for them to watch, Charlotte sorted through them all, and picked one called "The Lie Will Kill You- And Hurt You." Although she was not incredibly pleased that Patrice had picked an 18 film- even though she was not scared of anything- Charlotte let it go this one occasion.

Andrew smiled at what the movie was called, saying "I will go and shut the curtains, and turn off all the lights, and get the munchies ready."

Charlotte then thought of another bit of essential preparation "Somebody better let Shaky out for a wee before we start this film, so we don't have to pause it halfway through?"

Patrice stood up slowly and went to let Shaky out, but then she had an idea, "Why don't we just shut her in the conservatory, and shut the door to the living room, so she can go out when she wants to?"

Charlotte and Andrew both nodded in agreement, while Andrew put the film on and Charlotte and Patrice each got a pillow ready in case, they got scared watching it.

When the film was about halfway through, Charlotte sat up with a start, as she heard something at the back of the house. Charlotte felt genuinely scared now, so she paused the film and whispered to Andrew, "Darling, I am not being daft or anything, but can you hear something coming from the back room, I am sure I can hear some footsteps?"

Andrew nodded and went to see what was happening, and he saw a tall male figure, dressed in denim jeans and a crisp polo shirt. Giving out a sigh of relief, he puffed out his cheeks and hissed "Oh, it's you Paul, what are you doing here? You frightened the life out of us!" he chuckled nervously, "we are watching a horror film!"

Paul couldn't apologise enough, "I am so sorry to disturb you, but we couldn't get hold of any of you on the phone, we just wondered how everyone was, so I used my key to let myself in, to check up on Shaky, and to see how the house was."

Andrew forgot that Paul had a spare key, "Is everything okay though, and is Gabbie all right?"

Paul smiled at Andrew, "Yes she is fine, thank you for asking, but she is sat in the car waiting for me, we were just a bit worried in case Shaky needed to be let out for a wee, as we didn't know what was happening with you guys."

Andrew went back into the living room to let Charlotte and Patrice know that it was just Paul and Gabbie, "You will never guess who has turned up to check in on Shaky, it's only your parents."

Charlotte, also relieved, went straight into hostess mode. "Well, invite them in then, and they can join us in watching the film and help us finish the sweets if they want to."

Andrew went back to Paul, who was busy rubbing the dog's tummy. "Do you both want to join us in watching a horror film Patrice picked out? I don't think you will have too much trouble picking up the storyline!"

Paul smiled and went to fetch Gabbie from the car. When everyone was settled with drinks and snacks, Charlotte pressed play, and they settled down and watched the film. Shaky sneaked in and curled up on Patrice's lap.

CHAPTER 12

The next day, everyone was surprised to wake up on the sofa and armchairs, as they had talked late into the night, too scared to leave or go to bed. Andrew was the first person to wake up, being licked by Shaky, so he made a pot of tea for everyone and let Shaky out to investigate the garden.

After he had made a pot of tea, and let Shaky out, he filled the grill pan with bacon and sausages. He went into the living room, and gently woke everyone up. "Morning you lot! I have made us all a pot of tea, and there is a cooked breakfast on the go."

Charlotte looked a bit angry with herself. "Oh, thank you darling, you're a sweetheart, I can't believe we all crashed down here, instead of going to bed properly…but then again, I was a bit scared of going up on my own, and I didn't want to leave my parents or Patrice down here."

Once everyone had enjoyed a really filling breakfast, Paul and Gabbie headed off home, "Thanks for inviting us to watch the film with you lot last night, we enjoyed the horror, but we are wondering if there is a sequel, as it would be good to see what happens to them all at the end, as it ended up on a cliff hanger didn't it? Also thank you for the lovely breakfast, Andrew."

Andrew smiled at both Paul and Gabbie, "You're more than welcome, and not to worry- I have plugged in all the house phones we have got and put on my mobile if you need to get in touch with us. I was also wondering the same about the film, I will have to have a look later to see if there is a second one and I will let you know."

Paul smiled then he unlocked the car, but before they made their way down the garden path, they all had a group hug with each other before Paul and Gabbie headed home.

After Patrice's grandparents went home, she looked at her dad and said "Dad, can we take Shaky to the park again please, I want to see if he obeys my commands when I call her back to us, and also to give my legs a bit more exercise?"

Andrew looked at her with a smile on his face, "Of course we can, Pat-anything you want. It's good that you want to keep making your legs stronger, and before you know it, you will be running for GB in the Olympics!"

Patrice laughed at that. "Oh dad, you're so funny! I won't be able to do that, as I am not fast at running at all-, I get out of breath dead easy."

"While we are taking Shaky for a walk, why don't we take the DVD'S back to the shop, then we can have a look to see if they have a sequel to that horror film, and if they do, we can order that one as everyone seems to want to know what happens next, as it ended up on a cliff hanger?"

Charlotte had just finished washing up after breakfast, and she followed Andrew and Patrice back into the living room. "I am not going to come out with you guys today, as I think I am going to nip into work and catch up on a few things, if you don't mind?"

Andrew looked at Charlotte, "Whatever you think is best darling, that's fine with us as well. Here is £50, why don't you have a mooch around the shops and treat yourself to something nice? We will be fine I might take Patrice and Shaky out somewhere for the day."

Charlotte gave Andrew the biggest hug and a whopper of a kiss, "Thanks, darling, I know you're perfectly capable of looking after our daughter, I don't have any worries there. Just don't have too much fun without me!"

Everyone got ready to go out, and Patrice called out to the puppy, who was giving proper attention to the wonderful smells coming out of the kitchen bin. "Shaky, walkies time!" Once she heard her name, Shaky came running as quickly as she could, and was about to jump up on Patrice, but Charlotte had to stop her from jumping up in case she knocked Patrice over. Once clipped onto her lead, she just looked up excitedly, tail wagging, wondering what adventures the day would bring.

Once everyone was ready to leave the house, Charlotte checked everywhere was locked up securely, as there had been some thieves in the area, and she dreaded getting broken into as she had so much personal and expensive stuff that meant a lot to her.

They went their separate ways, Andrew taking Patrice and Shaky in the car for their first stop, the video store. Andrew quickly nipped in, leaving Patrice and Shaky in the car. When Andrew got to the cashier, he asked, "Excuse me I want to return these DVD'S, and is there a follow-up of 'The Lie Will Kill You and Hurt You,' please, as that one ended up as a cliff hanger, and we want to know what happens next."

The cashier called her colleague Robert, who had loads of tattoos, and was skinny, with a beard.

"Hi there, I know what you mean, it was good, and I admit also wanting to know what happens next, too. I will just check on our systems to see if there is another one."

After a few minutes of him searching the system, he gave an 'Aha.'

"You're in luck, there is another one, but unfortunately it's out at the moment; but once it's back in store, I can ring you and let you know and I can save it for you if you like, mate?"

Andrew replied, "Oh yes please, but can I ask what is the second one called? I might be able to find it somewhere else?"

Robert replied, with a smirk "They thought long and hard, and came up with 'The Lie Will Kill You- And Hurt You Worse.' Hope that's some help for you?"

"So, would it be ok for you to let me know when it's back in store please? Here's my number, the store clerk handed Robert a card and a pen and he quickly jotted down his digits and handed it over."

After Robert agreed to let Andrew know when the DVD was back in store, Andrew went back to the car, and they all headed out some place special where they could also let Shaky run free and wild in the woods.

While they were in the car on their travels, Patrice said, "Dad, where we off to, then?" Andrew glanced briefly at her and with a shrug replied, "I don't know yet, I am just driving round looking for inspiration, but where do you fancy going?"

Patrice had a few places in mind that she could have suggested, but she replied with a smile on her face, "I don't mind Dad, you can pick if you want to, but I know where we haven't been for a while- well not since I was a kid- we haven't been to Bluebottle Woods for ages, have we? It's nice and quiet up there, just fields."

Andrew risked another quick look at Patrice, and smiled back at her, trying not to betray his amusement at her thinking that her being a kid was so long ago.

"Well, we can go there if you want to; that might be a better place to give Shaky a bit more training, and we can get her more used to doing what you tell her."

Andrew went right round the roundabout to turn towards Bluebottle Woods, as he was going to go to a much nearer, more formal park, but he did think that this was a better idea, since at the woods Shaky would hardly need to be on a lead at all, and she could run and sniff as much as he wanted.

When they got to the woods, after a chatty journey spent re-living happy memories of when they last made this trip out, they had found a space in the car park. Andrew went to get a ticket from the machine while Patrice put Shaky on her lead, just to get her safely away from the cars.

Andrew looked at how happy Patrice was, "Darling, we only have an hour or so here I am afraid, it's getting late already, and I bet your mum will be home before too much longer- and sadly, it's my turn to cook tea tonight! I hope you don't mind?"

Patrice smiled at her dad, "Of course I don't mind, why, would I mind? It's just nice to be here again, I have not been here since I was a little girl."

Shaky was beyond excited in being here, in this wonderful new place, full of sights, sounds and smells that just had to be explored. She was barking and pulling on her lead so much that Andrew took over from Patrice in holding her under control. Andrew was concerned, quite apart from keeping the dog safe, that nothing happened to Patrice, who was even now still a bit unsteady on her feet.

Shaky started to calm down a bit once they got clear of the car park: she was still a bit nervous about being by unfamiliar cars and became a bit unpredictable. Among the trees, ploughing through the leaf litter, she relaxed into a thorough survey of the scent-scape around her.

Andrew looked at his daughter and said, "Do you want to try and hold her on the lead now, as she has calmed down a bit, then when we get to the top of the hill we can try and train her again and see if she listens to your commands?"

Patrice smiled at her dad, "Oh yes, please, Dad that would be great, she has to learn to obey me as well as you and Mum, doesn't she?"

Andrew smiled back, and they headed up to the top of the hill, guiding Shaky and her investigations in the right general direction. Shaky was doing quite well in not pulling Patrice too quickly, and she ended up enjoying holding her, which made a change, as she had until now been worried about holding her on the lead, in case she pulled so hard that she ended up sprawled on the ground.

While they walked up the hill, they met a nice old couple coming up from another path they also had a little dog which was only young, some sort of collie cross. They stopped to chat to each other, as dog owners often did. Andrew said, "Morning, what a lovely day it is today. What a cute dog you have, is it a boy or a girl?"

The lady, who was tall with long hair and big build replied, "It's he and his name is Toto, he's only a year old." Looking kindly down at Patrice the woman smiled warmly as she patted Shaky "Your dog is lovely as well, what is his or her name?"

Patrice replied with a smile on her face, as she liked meeting new people when out for a walk, "Her name is Shaky, and she's only a pup really, as I got her for my 16th birthday a few months ago, and we are still training her up."

 "Aww, she is so cute, she's Golden Retriever, isn't she?" Shaky and Toto were getting acquainted, too, sniffing with tails wagging.

Patrice and Andrew smiled and nodded and then they all carried on up the hill together, but before they reached the top, Patrice decided to let Shaky off his lead, to see if she behaved herself with Toto, who had been let off to have a play.

Patrice was relieved to see that she was well – behaved and delighted that she seemed to listen to everything Patrice told her to do. The little group stayed together for about ten minutes while Totos' mistress Wendy introduced her husband Callum, who seemed a bit shy. He looked a bit older than Wendy, and Wendy explained a bit about her husband, while he wandered off to see what the dogs were up to.

"Just to let you both know that Callum is not ignoring you, he's just not very sociable at the moment. We don't quite know what's wrong with him, and it is very worrying for me and our children as well."

Andrew looked incredibly sad at what he had just heard and replied, "I am so sorry to hear that, I bet it is very worrying; but we hope you get some answers from your doctors, or whoever you're speaking to. I don't mean to be rude or anything, but we need to move on I am afraid as my wife will be home in the next hour, and we still need to do our training with Shaky."

Wendy nodded and smiled and then called Toto to come to her, while Andrew did the same for Shaky. Once the dogs came back, bright eyed from all their fun, each little group of people and dog went their separate ways.

While Patrice, Andrew and Shaky were heading off to a clearing for the training exercises, Andrew had to put Shaky back on the lead, having seen a cat up ahead; he didn't want to risk Shaky losing all his discipline and running off in full chase. She was doing so well, and it would be a shame to spoil it.

Patrice had a puzzled look on her face, "Dad why did you put Shaky back on her lead? As she was doing ever so well by not running off and even listened to me when I told him to come back over to me?"

Andrew turned to face his daughter as he was walking fast, trying to buy a bit more time. "I have only put her back on her lead because I saw a cat up ahead, and I was not sure what she would have done if she saw it- she might have runway off, and we do have to be careful in these woods because of the farmer."

Patrice then saw the cat herself and she smiled back at her dad, "Oh I see the cat now, that's a good idea! I don't understand why we have to be careful because of the farmer, though? Is it because he doesn't like anyone on his property?"

Andrew nodded to his daughter then they carried on walking up the hill until they got to the top, where they found there were loads of horses in the next field, so they had to keep Shaky on the lead for a bit longer.

Patrice looked at her dad with a disappointed look. "If we cannot let Shaky off her lead, why don't we just turn back and go back home as it's getting late and dark now?"

Andrew agreed, and they turned around and started to head back to the car, but while they were walking down the hill, the bloke from the video store rang up, "Oh hello, Mr Umar, it's Robert here from the video store, just to let you know that the film you were asking about has just come back in, if you wanted me to save it till you come back in store."

Andrew had a big fat smile on his face, "I will nip in on the way home, if that's okay, as we are not far from where you are- we are just heading back to the car now."

Before they got back to the car, it started to hammer it down, so they had to rush the last few hundred yards as they didn't have waterproof jackets on, and they were getting soaked. Shaky did not seem too bothered.

CHAPTER 13

The next morning, after everyone had breakfast, the house phone started to ring, and Patrice went to answer it. It was her head teacher. "Oh, hello Patrice, how are you feeling today, is your mum or dad available to talk, please?"

Patrice passed the phone to her mum, as her dad was in the shower getting ready and trying to wake himself up a bit. "Mum, it's Mr Connel, he wants a quick word with you."

Once Patrice had handed the phone to her mum, Charlotte said, "Hi Mr Connel, hope you're well? Is everything okay?"

Mr Connel, who had been the head teacher for many years replied, "Yes everything is fine, we were just wondering when Patrice was coming back to school; that's all?"

Charlotte looked at Patrice with a smile on her face, but Patrice gave her mum a distinctly unhappy look back, "I will try and get Patrice to come back to school next week, if that's okay with you Mr Connel?"

After Charlotte got off the phone, she turned back to face Patrice, and said "Darling, I know you don't like school, but you need to go back sometime, and Mr Connel has said he will do everything he can to help you to get back into the swing of things at school. If I am being honest, school might be the best option for you next week; we can go in later today and have a word with him as he wants to talk to us both anyway before you go back."

Patrice wasn't incredibly happy about going back to school, but she knew she had to go back one day. With a sigh, and a shrug of her shoulders, "Okay, mum, we can go in today and talk to him."

Once Andrew was finished in the shower, Charlotte shouted up to him, "Darling, Mr Connel has just rung up, he wanted to know if we can pop in later today to speak to him, and I have said that Patrice can hopefully go back to school next week, as she needs to go back to school sooner rather than later - she has missed out on loads of school work while she has been off."

Andrew came down after he got dressed, so they could all get ready and head off to Patrice's school to talk to the head teacher.

Once they got to the school, they signed in with the secretary, and went to sit outside Mr. Connel's room.

One of the students who had been picking on Patrice came walking past, and started laughing in front of Patrice's face saying, "Hahaha, you can't walk properly and you're so ugly, you need to be in a zoo so everyone can see how ugly you are, and they can all laugh at you." Andrew and Charlotte were both shocked to see this behaviour for themselves, especially so since it happened right in front of them, as if they were not there.

Patrice exploded into tears and ran as best her legs could muster straight out of the school, desperate to escape the humiliation of the scene. She just couldn't stand being there any longer. Very soon after all of this had happened, Mr Connel came out, and gave Charlotte and Andrew a sorry look, "Hello Mr and Mrs Umar, thank you for coming in. May I ask where Patrice is, I was hoping that she would have come with you, so we can all have a chat together?"

Now it was Charlotte's turn to cry. "First of all, I am sorry for crying, but it was just so hard for me to see Patrice getting picked on right here, just now, right in front of us. The nasty girl was picking on her and telling her that she needs to be in the zoo where everyone will laugh at her because she is ugly. Is this how you expect your pupils to behave?

Mr Connel looked at Charlotte shocked, "I am so sorry to hear this, we have zero tolerance in this school for that sort of behaviour. I will certainly find the underlying cause of it; you have my word on that." Andrew gave him a quick description of the culprit, to make sure that he did.

Because Charlotte was so shaken up, Andrew was comforting her as he angrily explained to the head teacher the aftermath of his pupils' unforgivable behaviour. "Patrice has run off somewhere. I will see if she has her mobile on her, so I can ring her and ask her to come back. I will also go and check at the car as she might be waiting for us there." Charlotte sniffed into her handkerchief and waved him away to do just that.

Ringing Patrice's number as he rushed back to the car, Andrew found a hurriedly scrawled note under a windscreen wiper which read **"I AM SORRY, I CAN T COPE ANYMORE LOVE YOU BOTH LOTS THOUGH."**

As soon as Andrew read this note from his poor, distraught daughter, he gave up trying to get an answer from her and rang Charlotte instead. "Darling, we have a problem, Patrice has left us a note on the windscreen, saying she can't cope anymore, but she loves us both lots. I am really worried now. Can you ask Mr Connel if she hung around with anyone in particular at school, anyone at all, who might be able to help us track her down?"

After Charlotte got off the phone with Andrew, she started to scream and started to cry again as she had only just calmed down. Mr Connel said, "What's the matter Mrs Umar, have you found Patrice?"

Charlotte shouted back "No, my husband has not found her. She has left us a note on the car, saying that she was sorry and that she couldn't cope anymore, and that she loved me and my husband a lot- and now he can't find her, and we are frantic about her. Did she hang around with anyone at school, do you know, who might be able to help us find her?"

Mr Connel got straight onto the public address system which was connected to the whole school and made a terse announcement: "This is Mr Connel, addressing all students and staff. You need to stop everything you're doing; I need to call an emergency meeting in the hall. Can everyone please gather in the hall, immediately."

Mr Connel returned to Charlotte and handed her his business card. "I am going to get all members of staff and all the students at this school to do a search for your daughter. Please let your husband know what's going on. Don't worry, we will find her. Here is my mobile number. If you find her, can you let me know please?"

Realising that Mr. Connel could not really do much more, Charlotte headed back to the car, to meet back up with Andrew. They went in search for Patrice, looking high and low, and even went to the highest hill, overlooking the town, just to see if she had fled up there.

Andrew then had a thought, "Darling, just remembered- I have got a tracking app on Patrice's phone that I downloaded the other day for when she went back to school, so we could tell where she was in case, she was late. I will just check to see if it is turned on."

Frustratingly, Patrice didn't seem to have her phone on, so they couldn't tell where she was. Charlotte then said to Andrew in a harsh voice, "Why or why would you put a tracking app on her phone, she's 16 now and there is no time limit as such for when she comes home."

Andrew looked hurt and snapped back "I did this for her safety, as a bloke I go golfing with, his daughter got kidnapped while walking home from school, and he said having that tracker on her phone saved her life, as they found her later that day tied up in a garage somewhere."

Charlotte was aghast at what Andrew had just told her, "Why on earth didn't you tell me this, when you heard about what happened?"

Andrew looked at Charlotte with a sorry look on his face, "I didn't want to worry you or Patrice, that's why I didn't tell you." They fell into an uneasy silence.

After about half an hour or so of Charlotte and Andrews' fruitless search for Patrice, Charlotte's phone rang. It was the head teacher. "Hello Mrs Umar, it's Mr Connel ringing you to see if you have had any luck in finding Patrice yet? I have just finished assembly. I have got everyone out looking for her. There was one friend of Patrice's who came forward, called Nicky, she told me that she is friends with your daughter, but they don't have each other's number, since they only talk during school time. Sadly, they don't normally hang out with each other apart from when they are walking to and from the school bus."

Charlotte started sobbing again. "Okay, thank you, we appreciate it so much; it's a shame that Patrice and Nicky don't hang out with each other during breaks or anything, because then we would know where Patrice might be hiding."

Once Charlotte got off the phone to Mr Connel, Charlotte and Andrew drove out to the woods where the previous afternoon had been so enjoyable. They eventually found Patrice hiding in some bushes at the edge of the car park, crying her eyes out and with a young man they didn't recognise.

Andrew shouted as loudly as he could, "WHAT THE HELL DO YOU THINK YOU'RE DOING WITH MY DAUGHTER! SHE IS ONLY 16 YEARS OLD! GET AWAY FROM HER THIS SECOND OR GOD HELP ME!"

Charlotte had to quickly ring Mr Connel, "Can you come quick please, we are in the woods, and we have found Patrice and she's with a lad who looks like he's 19 or so and I think my husband is going to do something not very nice to this lad."

Within five minutes of Charlotte ending the call, Mr Connel and a few other members of male staff turned up to make sure that Andrew didn't do anything bad.

One of the teachers called Mr Longbottom who was a boxing teacher at the school grabbed Mr Umar quickly before he could grab the young lad who was tall and had loads of tattoos all over his body.

Andrew shouted at Mr Longbottom, "Please get of me, I am not going to hit him, but either of you teachers know this lad? As I think his parents need to know that he's trying to get in my little girl's pants and if he belongs to this school, I think he needs to be expelled."

Another member of staff who was also there called Mr Blue-Bottom replied, "Yes, I know him as he's my son and he is already expelled from this school, and he should be at home as he is supposed to be looking after my sick wife not doing this sort of thing."

Mr Blue- Bottom grabbed the lad's arm and dragged him away from Patrice and her parents and started hitting him around the head loads of times.

CHAPTER 14

The next day, after everything that had gone off, Andrew decided to ring the school so he could talk to Mr Bottom and apologise about his actions yesterday and to make sure that Patrice wouldn't get kicked out of school because of his behaviour.

"Excuse me is that Mr Connel? My name is Mr Umar and I am ringing to say I am sorry to Mr Blue bottom and to the other members of staff as well for my actions yesterday it was just a shock to see my daughter with a lad who is older than she is and I also want to make sure that Patrice won't get expelled for my actions as it's her exams coming up soon and she needs to be back in school so she can do some practise tests as well."

After Andrew said what he had to say on the phone Mr Connel replied, "I would be in the same boat as you were yesterday if I had a young daughter about Patrice's age. But I will pass on the message if you want me to, now that Patrice is home safe, and sound shall we make a date for another meeting and talk about what plans me and the other teachers can put in place for when she returns as her GCSE'S are quickly approaching and she needs to come and do some mock tests with her class in a few weeks' time?"

Andrew agreed and replied, "We don't have anything planned for today so we can come in the next hour or so if that's any help to you, but I just hope that there won't be anyone who will pick on my daughter while we are waiting to see you in your office."

After Andrew got off the phone with Mr Connel, Patrice looked at her dad with a sad face, "Dad, why do I have to go with you as I will only bump into someone else who don't like me and who will pick on me a bit more."

Andrew started to cry a bit as he never cried in front of his daughter, "Darling you need to be there as its about you as its coming up to exams and you need to find out what you have missed out on, don't worry Mr Connel has said we can wait inside his office for him if he is not there but he is going to make sure he will be there so you won't get picked on again."

Patrice went to get her coat on while Charlotte and Andrew went to sit in the car ready to head to Patrice's school, but this time before they got there, Charlotte rings Mr Connels' office phone to see if he's there so they don't have to wait outside his office in case the same incident happened again.

Just before they turned round the bend, Charlottes phone rings just when she was in the middle of pressing some numbers in, "Oh hello Mr Connel, I was just about to ring you to make sure that you're in the office as we are just around the corner now as Patrice is scared in case we have to wait outside your office."

Mr Connel replied, "That is why I am ringing you; we have just had an emergency with some of the pupils in a classroom and I will be about ten minutes late but my receptionist knows that you're on the way and she will let you into my office so you can sit and wait in there for me to finish this emergency off."

Charlotte replied with a smile on her face, "Thank you so much, but if you prefer, we can rearrange although its best to talk about Patrice today as its coming up to her exams and she needs to do some practising but me and my husband can't do it as we are not teachers, and we don't know the answers as its all changed since we were at school."

Mr Connel replied, "No its fine we can still have the meeting, as yes you are right it is coming up to exams and Patrice does need to do some practise exams with her class to see how she gets on."

Once Charlotte put the phone down, she turned and looked at her husband, "Mr Connel still wants us to go and have this meeting with him, but he has to deal with an emergency first so he said he might be ten minutes late and that his receptionist knows we are coming so she will let us into his office to wait in there for him. I just hope he isn't longer than ten minutes but things like this can't be helped really."

Once they arrived at the school, they all walked up the hill to get to the main building where Mr Connels' office was and they went to sign in and the receptionist let them into his office to go and wait in there and said, "Mr Connel has just rung me up to say he won't be long now, did you want anything to drink while you wait?"

Everyone shook their heads and said, "No thank you we have just had a drink but thank you anyway."

While they were all waiting in his office, Patrice couldn't sit still, and she ended up going to the toilet about five times before Mr Connel came back to his office.

When Patrice came back into the office, she shut the door behind her, and they had a conversation for about an hour or so about Patrice's learning and how she was getting on with walking. Mr Connel decided to ask Patrice, "You while you are here, did you want to do a quick practise exam while I talk to your parents alone, please?"

Patrice didn't know what to say and she looked shocked, "That might not be a bad idea if you think that it might help me a bit more, but I don't understand why you have to talk to my parents without me?"

Mr Connel, went into his cabinet and found a practise paper that she could have a look over and to have a go at, "I will check over it for you once you have finished the paper if that's ok just to see what stage you will be at because you have missed so much while you have been off school I will go and unlock the room next door for you to go in and have a go at the paper."

Patrice nodded and followed Mr Connel into the room next door, "I will give you an hour to have a go at this paper and once the hour is up, I will come and get you if that's ok with you?"

Patrice nodded and she started to have a go at the practise paper while the head teacher went back to his office and had a word with Charlotte and Andrew. "Mr and Mrs Umar I was just wondering how Patrice was getting on at home with walking and everything as I bet it was a shock for you all what happened to her. We want to do the best we can to help Patrice to get back into the swing of things back at school."

Charlotte replied, "Yes, she is doing a lot better at walking now, sometimes she even wants to take her puppy out for a walk by herself at times as she feels a lot more motivated as well, but she still has to do some physio on her legs."

Andrew then spoke up as he had some concerns for when she came back to school because of what happened the other day, "You know when she comes back to school, will she be in the same class as them bullies who were picking on her the other day as I think something really needs to be done about that as most days when she was at school, she either came home crying or her clothes were mucky from people throwing things at her?"

Mr Connel looked horrified at what he just heard, "I am so sorry that Patrice had to go through that ordeal while she was here but let me reassure you that I will be keeping a close eye on her when she returns, and I will personal make sure that whoever is picking on Patrice will be dealt with immediately."

After an hour of Patrice doing the practise test, Mr Connel went next door to see how she was doing and noticed that she was crying, "What up Patrice? Why are you crying? How are you getting on with the practise paper as the hour has gone now, can you put your pen down please and come back into my office so we can check over what you have done?"

Patrice turned to face Mr Connel, "I struggled a bit with the practise paper but I managed to finish it, and the reason I am crying is because Susie came into the room a she saw you putting me in here and started calling me names and she even gave me a black eye and when I was on the floor she was kicking me in my stomach and calling me because I still cannot walk properly and then she sneaked some of her other mates in here while no one else was looking and they were all punching me."

Mr Connel couldn't believe what had just happened and he went over to where she was sitting, "Oh Patrice I am so sorry this happened to you, I hope this does not put you back, so you struggle walking now. Let me reassure you that this will not be happening again, and I will exclude them for doing this to you let's get you back into my office and we will go over the practise exam you have just done."

They headed back into the office, where Charlotte and Andrew noticed that Patrice was crying and that she was walking unsteady again, "Oh darling what's the matter why are you unsteady on your legs again?"

Patrice went straight over to her parents, "While I was next door, this girl who keep picking on me called Susie saw me in here, and she sneaked in and started beating me up and then kicking me and her mates came in also and they did the same thing."

Andrew looked horrified and said, "Right we are taking you straight back to the hospital for you to get checked over but can I ask a favour please Mr Connel, can you make sure this will get sorted out ASAP please before she returns back to school and I am sorry but we cannot stay here any longer once you have looked over the practise test, can you ring us up please and let us know how she did please as we really need to get her checked out."

Mr Connel nodded in agreement as she was already on the phone ringing Susie's parents, and he was going to look for Susie and her friends to find the underlying cause of why they did this and to exclude them all from school.

CHAPTER 15

The morning, after the meeting with Mr Connel, they discovered what happened to their daughter when she was in the next room.

While they were having breakfast there was a knock on the door and Andrew goes to answer it, "Oh morning Mr Connel what do we owe this visit as thought you was going to ring us when you had marked the paper?"

Mr Connel smiled at Andrew and replied, "I thought while I was in the neighbourhood checking up on children who are skiving from school, I thought I would come in and check on how Patrice was doing today after the incident yesterday and to also talk to you all about her results from the mock exam she did yesterday."

Andrew looked at his family and replied, "Please do come in, I am just about to make a cup of tea if you want to join us while you talk to us about the results of Patrice's mock exam."

Donald wiped his feet and said hello to everyone then he went into the living room where Charlotte and Patrice were sitting, "Good morning, Mrs Umar and Patrice hope your both doing well. I have just explained to your husband the reason why I have come today and don't worry its nothing bad or anything as I was just in the area and thought I would pop over and see how you're all doing after yesterday and to talk about Patrice's mock exam results as well."

Charlotte smiled at Donald and replied, "Do sit down please Mr Connel, has my husband asked if you wanted a drink or anything?"

Donald smiled and replied, "Like I have just said to your husband please called me Donald but Patrice while you're not in school you can also call me by my first name but while you're in school you call me Mr Connel."

Patrice laughed and replied, "Off course I will Donald just wanted to thank you also for the chat we had in the other room yesterday when you saw me crying."

Donald replied while he was also laughing, "Your more than welcome as that is part of my job as well to make sure all of my students are ok and feel safe in school. Now that is sorted, can we talk about your mock exam you did yesterday please?"

Everyone agreed but before they started to talk about the mock exam, Charlotte asked, "Donald do you fancy some cheesecake as I have made my special cheesecake and there is plenty to go around if you want a piece as these two always fight over my cheesecake as they cannot get enough."

Donald smiled and Charlotte went to grab everyone a slice of the lovely cheesecake that she made yesterday. While they were eating the cheesecake, Donald said, "I have some good and some bad news to tell you about the mock exam, first of all, Patrice you did really well on your English Literature but on your maths, I am afraid you didn't pass that and I have been told while you're doing your PE lessons you struggle doing certain things that most people can do easily like catching and throwing a ball to someone when you're playing like netball as I have spoken to other members of staff about your skills and some of them don't understand why that is."

Charlotte and Andrew looked puzzled, and Charlotte said, "So does this mean that she has Dyspraxia because I have been wondering about that since a conversation with a lady whose child has similar difficulties?

Donald looked a bit sad at giving them this news and replied, "Well the results show she has mild learning difficulties.

Charlotte said that Patrice did take an exceedingly long time to learn to tie her shoelaces, hop, skip, and ride a bike when she was younger, and I did wonder why"

Donald then replied that she would receive extra support in lessons. Charlotte breathed a sigh of relief but knew there was something more than just mild learning difficulties and resolved to do further research.

Patrice also looked shocked, "I wonder if that's why I am getting picked on a lot because I am not brainy enough like everyone else and I take a long time in finishing things like if we are running on the running field etc?"

Donald then shook everyone hands, "Well I am sorry, but I will have to get back to the school now as its nearly time for the older children to do their exams and I need to be there to make sure that no one cheats."

Everyone said goodbye to Donald then he headed out of the door to his car then he left.

CHAPTER 16

The next morning after everything what happened everyone still couldn't get their heads around what Donald had told them. When Patrice got downstairs, she said to her mum, "Mum why am I so thick? Why can't I just be a normal person like everyone else as I hate being a loner with no friends or anything? Also, I woke up with some pain in my side and my legs as I was doing ever so well until Susie and her friends beat me up the other day, I can hardly walk well no more as I keep feeling like I am going to fall over, and I keep going dizzy and weak."

Charlotte got straight onto the phone to the hospital again and explained everything that happened when she was in a different room doing her mock test for school and that a few girls were beating her up.

While Charlotte was talking to Margaret who was Patrice's nurse while she was in hospital Margaret replied, "Oh I am sorry to hear what happened to Patrice while she was in a different room from you and your husband while she was doing her mock exam, did you want to bring her in today and I can give her another check over to see what we can do to help."

Charlotte looked at Andrew and replied, "Yes please that would be perfect we will come straight away as I wouldn't forgive myself if anything happened to Patrice and we didn't help her."

Charlotte looked at Patrice, "Right Patrice I have just got off the phone with Margaret who was looking after you while you were in hospital, and she suggested that we take you back to hospital straight away to get you checked over so can you go and get ready please darling."

Patrice nodded as she knew that she had to get checked over to see what's wrong with her, "Ok mum I will go and get ready as I hate feeling unwell, I just hope I don't have to stay in again."

Charlotte followed Patrice upstairs so she could pack a few things just in case she had to stay in as Patrice went to have a quick shower even though she was in pain as she wanted to be all nice and clean for when the nurse saw her.

While Patrice was in the shower, she had to shout her mum as she was struggling in washing herself, "Mum can you come in the bathroom for a moment please as I am struggling to wash as I am in so much pain and I am struggling even more in walking and everything."

Charlotte shouts down to her husband "Darling I think we might have to ring for an ambulance as Patrice is struggling doing everything again and I am so worried about her. Also, I will need to ring Mr Connel to let him know what has happened so he can let them nasty bullies know what they have done to Patrice as she was doing ever so well but now, they have put her back again."

Andrew gets straight onto the phone to 999, "Hello can we have an ambulance straight away please as it's my daughter and she has only been out of hospital for a few months but now she's complaining she is in pain again and is struggling in doing her normal everyday things."

The operator replied, "I know this is a stressing time for you all again at the moment, but please can you let your wife know that we have arranged for an ambulance to come to your home address straight away and can you stay on the line until it arrives, please sir."

While Andrew was on the phone, Charlotte carried on washing her daughter and trying to help her to get out of the shower, but Patrice couldn't do it at all so Charlotte said, "Darling I know you're in pain, but can you please try for me and get out of the shower so we can put some clothes on you for when the ambulance arrives."

Patrice started to cry as she hated this as she hated relying on her mum to help her to get washed, "Mum

I can't get out of the bathtub at all I can sit down in the bathtub, and you can dry me off in here and then put a nightie on me?"

Charlotte shouted to Andrew, "Any news on the ambulance?"

After five minutes of Andrew being on the phone, the ambulance turns up as they were on red lights as it was an emergency.

The paramedic said, "Thank you for letting us in, don't worry we will try our best to help your daughter. Andrew had explained where the bathroom was, and they went straight up.

"Is she on any medications or anything?" Andrew shook his head while the paramedics went over to where Patrice was in the bathroom and fitted breathing equipment onto her.

"It looks like we will have to take her down to Harbour General and get her booked in, but I am afraid there is only 1 person allowed in the back of the ambulance with us."

Since Charlotte went in the ambulance with Patrice last time, Andrew went in the ambulance with his daughter and Charlotte drove her car there.

While they were all waiting for the doctor to come and see Patrice, Andrew got on his phone to see where Charlotte was, "Darling are you far away? As I was thinking we could do some more research into what Patrice has got which is Dyspraxia, but you have the laptop in your car."

Charlotte was shaking as she was driving her car, "I am just in the carpark now, I forgot I had the laptop in the bot of my car, and yes I agree we do need to do some more research on Dyspraxia to see what sort of help we can give her at home."

When Charlotte arrived on the ward, she managed to log into the hospitals Wi-Fi and Charlotte logged in to her laptop and they both looked into Dyspraxia to see what sort of help they could give their daughter at home.

Charlotte's research pointed towards Dyspraxia and after numerous telephone calls and meetings at school and with no further support being offered, she contacted the Dyspraxia Foundation.

This conversation confirmed that all Patrice's gross and finer motor skills were due to Dyspraxia and as school was denying that Patrice needed any further help, she contacted a private educational psychologist and paid for her to be assessed. The consultant said that Patrice has severe learning difficulties and Dyspraxia and that he was disgusted that the school had offered no further support and advised Charlotte to take the school to court for not adequately addressing Patrice's educational needs, that, in fact, she should have been statemented.

Once home, Charlotte made further phone calls and told the school secretary that she would supply school with a copy of the private educational psychological assessment once she received it, which she did and that if they did not Statement Patrice, she would be taking the school to court for neglect.

School arranged for Patrice to be assessed by the educational authorities own educational psychologist who said Patrice had mild learning difficulties but did not need statementing. Charlotte was shocked and incredulous because now there was only 6 months to go until Patrice's exams, so after attending further meetings with school, writing more letters to the Educational Authority, and making even more phone calls, she contacted the solicitor recommended by the private educational psychologist.

The solicitor agreed that there was a case to be had against the educational authority. When Charlotte told her that she had kept diaries since she was 14 years of age which included shorthand notes about Patricie's milestones and difficulties and what she was told at every parents evening since Patrice was 6 when Charlotte would make her concerns known about the difficulties she had when helping Patrice with her homework, and such things as trying to teach her the recorder, etc, the Solicitor asked her to transcribe these into longhand.

The Solicitor collected all the phone messages; letters written by Charlotte to school; communications from school to Charlotte; all the workbooks Charlotte had purchased to try to help Patrice with maths, spellings and English, plus educational assessments etc. However, after 2 years she said that although it was clear that Patrice should have been statemented much earlier in school life, they could not take the school to court because there was no evidence to show that the school had caused Patrice any educational harm.

This was because Charlotte had paid for Patrice to attend the Learnwrite centre where she was helped with her writing and fine motor skills & also where she was also diagnosed with dyscalcula and was supported with that.

She also spent so much time trying to educate Patrice herself (which was beneficial to Patrice but unfortunately damaging for the court case) which meant that Patrice was not struggling as much as she could have been without Charlotte's help, even though she left school with grades of mostly F's, G's along with ungraded.

CHAPTER 17

The next day, after all the research that Charlotte did for Patrice, with her Dyspraxia and trying to help her to get her strength back up and also her confidence, Patrice asked, "Mum can we try and do something today please just me and you since dad is busy working today as I always do something with dad, and I hardly ever get to spend time with you?"

Charlotte looked at Patrice with a big grin on her face, "I was hoping that you would have asked me that one day, as you always spend time with your dad but hardly any time with me, but I guess that's because you're a daddy's girl and not a mummy's girl so off course we can spend the day together."

Patrice went to get a quick shower and to get changed out of her nightclothes, so she was ready to go out for the day with her mum, "Mum where are we going so, I know what sort of clothes to put on or I am deciding where we are going?"

Charlotte shouted up the stairs to her daughter, "Did you want me to choose somewhere then? If so, I will have a think about it while you're in the shower."

After Patrice got out of the shower she shouted down, "Mum have you decided where we are going yet, please as I need to know what sort of clothes to wear?"

Charlotte replied from her bedroom, "Put whatever you want on as I still don't know where we are going yet, but I do have a few ideas but what do you want to do darling?"

Patrice had a long hard think about what she wanted to do with her mum, "I seriously don't know mum, why don't we just play it by ear?"

Charlotte and Patrice carried on getting ready to go out somewhere, but they didn't know where to go until Patrice had an idea, "Why don't we go to the cinema as there is a good film that's just come out called The Mist which sounds really good but think it's an 18 but I will be allowed to watch it with you?"

Charlotte had a long hard think about it while she was brushing her hair and putting makeup on, "I suppose we can go and watch that if you really want to since you also watched that horror film with us the other week."

Patrice couldn't actually believe that her mum agreed to taking her to see an 18 movie, "Thanks mum I so can't wait to go and watch this with you as I have heard it's really good."

Once they were both ready, Charlotte feed Shaky and they both headed out to the car. But just before they drove off, Charlotte decided to check on her phone to see if the cinema was showing that film before, they got there as they didn't want a wasted journey. "Darling we are in luck they are showing that film today but not till later this afternoon, but if you want, we can go for something to eat first at the pub and make a day of this and I will let your dad know to make his own tea if we are not back in time."

Patrice nodded and then Charlotte started the car for them to go to a pub which wasn't far from the cinema called "The Love Boat" and actually it was just right around the corner from the cinema which was called the underground cinema.

When they managed to park the car, Patrice said, "Mum did you want me to go and get us a table as the car park looks quite full, and we might not be able to get a table."

Charlotte nodded at her daughter then she went in the pub and found a table and Patrice ordered two cokes from the bar while her mum was parking up.

She also spent so much time trying to educate Patrice herself (which was beneficial to Patrice but unfortunately damaging for the court case) which meant that Patrice was not struggling as much as she could have been without Charlotte's help, even though she left school with grades of mostly F's, G's along with ungraded.

CHAPTER 17

The next day, after all the research that Charlotte did for Patrice, with her Dyspraxia and trying to help her to get her strength back up and also her confidence, Patrice asked, "Mum can we try and do something today please just me and you since dad is busy working today as I always do something with dad, and I hardly ever get to spend time with you?"

Charlotte looked at Patrice with a big grin on her face, "I was hoping that you would have asked me that one day, as you always spend time with your dad but hardly any time with me, but I guess that's because you're a daddy's girl and not a mummy's girl so off course we can spend the day together."

Patrice went to get a quick shower and to get changed out of her nightclothes, so she was ready to go out for the day with her mum, "Mum where are we going so, I know what sort of clothes to put on or I am deciding where we are going?"

Charlotte shouted up the stairs to her daughter, "Did you want me to choose somewhere then? If so, I will have a think about it while you're in the shower."

After Patrice got out of the shower she shouted down, "Mum have you decided where we are going yet, please as I need to know what sort of clothes to wear?"

Charlotte replied from her bedroom, "Put whatever you want on as I still don't know where we are going yet, but I do have a few ideas but what do you want to do darling?"

Patrice had a long hard think about what she wanted to do with her mum, "I seriously don't know mum, why don't we just play it by ear?"

Charlotte and Patrice carried on getting ready to go out somewhere, but they didn't know where to go until Patrice had an idea, "Why don't we go to the cinema as there is a good film that's just come out called The Mist which sounds really good but think it's an 18 but I will be allowed to watch it with you?"

Charlotte had a long hard think about it while she was brushing her hair and putting makeup on, "I suppose we can go and watch that if you really want to since you also watched that horror film with us the other week."

Patrice couldn't actually believe that her mum agreed to taking her to see an 18 movie, "Thanks mum I so can't wait to go and watch this with you as I have heard it's really good."

Once they were both ready, Charlotte feed Shaky and they both headed out to the car. But just before they drove off, Charlotte decided to check on her phone to see if the cinema was showing that film before, they got there as they didn't want a wasted journey. "Darling we are in luck they are showing that film today but not till later this afternoon, but if you want, we can go for something to eat first at the pub and make a day of this and I will let your dad know to make his own tea if we are not back in time."

Patrice nodded and then Charlotte started the car for them to go to a pub which wasn't far from the cinema called "The Love Boat" and actually it was just right around the corner from the cinema which was called the underground cinema.

When they managed to park the car, Patrice said, "Mum did you want me to go and get us a table as the car park looks quite full, and we might not be able to get a table."

Charlotte nodded at her daughter then she went in the pub and found a table and Patrice ordered two cokes from the bar while her mum was, I am parking up.

After Patrice had ordered the drinks, she went to find a table for her and her mum to sit at and while she was waiting for her mum to come in, she had a quick look at the menu to see what she fancied to eat.

While Patrice was looking at the menu, she notices someone from her school called Angel coming straight over to her, "Oh I didn't realise it was tramp day in here today we had better go someplace else

Nick as we don't want to be linked with tramps do, we darling?"

But while Angel was saying these nasty horrible things to Patrice, Charlotte comes over to them, "Excuse me miss, you better leave my daughter alone as we don't want to be linked with two snobs who think they are better than everyone else and I am sure I know who your parents are as well."

Angel looked shocked, "Oh I am quacking in my shoes as my parents don't care about me and they won't do anything anyway, but you can talk to my parents if you want to if that would make you feel any better Haha."

After a few minutes of Angel and her fella standing right over Patrice and her mum, the manager of the bar comes over, "Sorry to disturb you mam, but are these young kids bothering you as they do cause trouble in here with my other customers and I have lost count the number of times I have asked them to leave and barred them, but they keep coming back."

Charlotte laughed, "No don't worry sir, I have delt with nutters in my life so its ok but thank you for your concern."

After the manager had gone and left Charlotte and Patrice to their own devices, they both had a look at the menu to see what they fancied to eat, "I fancy

Lamb Shank as I have never had that before I think mum if that's ok with you? But what are you having to eat?"

Charlotte had a proper look at the menu, "I can't decide so I think I might have the same as you darling. I will just go up to the bar and order the food for us."

After an hour of them waiting for their meals to turn up the waitress comes over to them "I am sorry its late but one of our head chefs ended up fainting in the kitchen and he never told us he was not well but for the inconvenient this has given you my manager said you can have the meal on us and he will give you a full refund when you go back up to the bar and he will also give you two free drinks as well."

Patrice checked online for her mum to see if they will have time to go to the pictures now, "I have some sad news mum, its saying online just now that all the seats for the show we wanted to go and see have all sold out now. But to be honest I don't mind as I have enjoyed today apart from that nasty girl from school picking on me."

CHAPTER 18

The next morning, Patrice woke up dead weird and was throwing up all night, "Mum are you ok as I don't feel too good and wondered if it was to do with the Lamb Shank, we both had yesterday?"

Charlotte rushed into Patrice's bedroom, "Oh darling I am sorry to hear that you're not feeling too good, you do look a bit pale let me just check your temperature for you as I am fine."

Charlotte rushed downstairs and went to find the first aid box they have somewhere in the kitchen, "Darling I have found the thermometer I will be back up in a minute to check your temperature."

Charlotte ran up the stairs back up to Patrice's room, "Darling can you lift your fringe up for me please so I can check your temperature."

Once Charlotte checked the readings on the thermometer, "your fine as the reading is saying your 36c which is normal the Lamb Shank might not off agreed with you as you have never had it before have you? Do you want to bring your blanket down with you and sit on the sofa all day and you and your dad can watch films all day if you want to?"

Patrice nodded and grabbed her blanket and made her way downstairs so she could go and join her dad in the living where he was doing some work on his laptop.

Charlotte went to fetch a sick bucket in case Patrice felt sick again as she didn't want her to rush to the toilet to be sick and probably end up fainting or anything. "Right darling I have to go into work for a few hours, but I will keep my phone on in case you need anything bringing back from the shops and I know your dads here but if you need anything at all just ring or text me ok."

Patrice nodded then Charlotte gave her and Andrew a kiss then she went off to work even though she hated leaving Patrice while she was not well.

Andrew looked away from his laptop, "Morning darling your mother said you're not very well and that you're spending the day on the sofa do you want one of my famous hot chocolates with some marshmallows on top?"

Patrice looked at her dad and gave him the biggest smile she could manage while she wasn't very well, "Yes please daddy I love your hot chocolates as for some reason you make them better than what mum does."

Andrew saved the work he did so far on his laptop then went into the kitchen and made his daughter a hot chocolate with some marshmallows on top.

While Andrew was in the kitchen Shaky comes and lies next to Patrice as he could tell that she wasn't very well. Once Andrew comes back in, he was shocked to see that Shaky was lying next to Patrice on the carpet and Patrice had fallen asleep. "I am sorry to wake you Pat, but I didn't want your hot chocolate getting cold." Patrice smiled at her dad, "Its ok father I don't mind you waking me up as I didn't even know I dropped off."

Andrew sat next to his daughter, and they drank their hot chocolate's together while they watched a bit of daytime telly.

After half an hour of Patrice drinking her drink, Charlotte pops back for her lunch to see how Patrice was doing, but when she walks through the door, she only saw Andrew "Hay darling how are you? You getting on ok with working from home today and how's our little girl?"

Andrew turned around to face Charlotte, "Oh hay what are you doing back I thought you took some sandwiches with you for dinner today? Patrice is fine but she's fast asleep on the sofa and I didn't want to wake her up to tell her to go to bed. But she seems a bit better now."

Charlotte headed to the kitchen to make some dinner and while she was in there Andrew followed her in,

"Do you want me to make you something nice for your dinner if you need to head back to work? Also, I was thinking, and only if you want to did you want to try for another baby as I think Patrice would love a brother or a sister to look after?"

Charlotte stopped what she was doing and started to cry, "Oh darling I have something to tell you, but I don't want to tell you anything without Patrice being awake, do you think you would go and wake her for me please as I have got something to tell you both."

Andrew nodded his head and went to go and gently wake his daughter up, "Patrice sorry for waking you as you looked so peaceful, but your mums come back for some dinner, and she wanted me to wake you up as she has something to tell us both and she didn't want to tell us separately."

Patrice gently woke up and they both headed into the kitchen where Charlotte was making some lunch, "Right you two I have something important to tell you and I didn't want to tell you both separately. I lied this morning about where I was going as I wanted to make sure before I told you both and you might want to sit down for this. I am pregnant and I am about two months gone as I went to see Doctor Gadin this morning to get some tests done as I have been feeling a bit under the weather recently and he told me what I already thought."

Andrew looked shocked and happy at the same time, "Oh wow darling that's great news I am so happy right now, but thought you was on the pill or something?"

Charlotte didn't know what to say, "I was on the pill but that is not always 100% protective. How do you feel Patrice?"

Patrice ran straight up to her mum, "I am overjoyed mum I can't wait to be a big sister I will always protect my brother or sister."

Andrew made them all a cup of tea while Charlotte and Patrice went back into the living room to watch some tv. "Mum, do you think we can watch The Lie Will Kill You and Hurt You Worse tonight please and can we invite grandma and grandad over to watch it with us as they liked the first one."

Charlotte nodded and Patrice went to find the phone quickly and rang her grandparents up, "Hi grandad you and grandma, ok? I don't suppose your busy tonight, are you? As we are going to watch The Lie Will Kill You and Hurt You Worse tonight which is the next one from what we saw the other week and I knew you liked the first one and wondered if you wanted to join us in watching it?"

Paul went quiet for a moment while he checked what they were doing, "You have yourself a deal Patrice but this time me and your grandma will bring the sweets this time since your mother brought them last time, we will get to yours for 9pm as you know your grandma loves her soaps."

After all the soaps had been on, there was a knock on the door and Charlotte went to go and answer it, "Hi mum and dad, so glad you could come round tonight and watch the film with us."

Gabbie smiled at her daughter "Off cause we wouldn't miss this for the world darling as the last one had me on the end of my seat and I wanted to know what happened next."

Paul and Gabbie went straight in, and they hung there coats up and took their shoes off as Charlotte had brought her parents some slippers to keep at her house as she hated people wearing shoes inside and she even had a note on the door to ask people to take off their shoes at the door so they wouldn't mess her carpet up.

Once everyone was sat down on the sofa, Andrew looked at Charlotte with a big fat grin on his face, "Darling are you going to give your parents the good news? Also, who wants a cup of tea or coffee or even my famous hot chocolate?"

Patrice looked at her father with a smile on her face, "Dad you know what I want as I can't get enough of your hot chocolates."

Gabbie and Paul both looked at Andrew with the same smile that Patrice gave her dad, "Can we try one of your famous hot chocolates please Andrew?"

Andrew went into the kitchen to make everyone a hot chocolate and Charlotte looked at her parents, "Mum dad I have something exciting to tell you and I don't know how to say this but you're going to be grandparents again."

Gabbie couldn't believe what she was hearing as if she remembered just before she gave birth to Patrice Gabbie was certain that she said she didn't want any more kids because of all the troubles she had when she was giving birth to Patrice.

Gabbie turned to look at her daughter, "Darling didn't you say after you had Patrice that you were going on the pill as you had a long and hard birth with your daughter that you didn't want to have any more kids again in case anything bad happened again while you were giving birth?"

Charlotte looked at her mum with a sad face, "Yes, I am on the pill, but they are not always 100% and you can still get pregnant while you're on the pill and yes,

I do remember saying that, but I don't understand why you're not over the moon for me and Andrew?"

Gabbie went over to Charlotte and gave her a big hug, "Off course I am happy for the pair of you, but I was just going by what you were saying to me after you had our lovely granddaughter 16 years ago. I better get my knitting needles out of the loft again and start to do some knitting."

Once Andrew brought everyone's drink in, Charlotte pressed play on the film, and they all sat still, and the women had cushions with them in case they got scared again and they could put them in front of their faces so they couldn't see what was happening.

After two hours of them all watching the film, and eating loads of sweets it was nearly midnight and Andrew looked at his in laws and said, "Do you both want to stay the night again as its nearly midnight and I don't want you driving back in the dark as you don't know whose around at this time of night?"

Paul looked back at Andrew with a smile on his face, "Only if you and Charlotte are ok with us staying as I know what you mean because the other week our neighbour was coming back at midnight and while he was getting out of his car in his drive way, this bloke came up to him with his face covered up and tried to mug him after he beat him up so badly that he ended up in hospital as he broke his rib."

Andrew and Charlotte looked shocked, and Charlotte went to go and hug her dad "Oh dad, I am so sorry that happened to your neighbour do you know how he is now? and I do hope you both stay with us tonight as I don't want the same happening to you or mum."

Gabbie looked at both Charlotte and Andrew, "I would love to stay overnight because what happened to our neighbour has made me scared of being out late and especially in the dark, I better let my neighbour know we are staying at yours and to go and put the temporary lights on, so people think we are at home, so no one tries to burglar us."

CHAPTER 19

The next morning, Patrice got up and made everyone some breakfast which was pancakes with maple syrup and she also made a pot of tea for everyone as well. "Breakfast is served everyone come and get it."

Everyone went into the kitchen and found that Patrice had been to the shop before she made breakfast, got some lovely flowers, and placed them in the middle of the kitchen table and she also brought her mum and grandma some flowers as well just to say thanks for everything they had done, and she also brought her dad and her grandad a lottery ticket each as well just to say thanks for everything.

Charlotte looked gobsmacked, "Oh this looks lovely darling, but you didn't have to go to this much trouble I can't wait to get stuck in."

While everyone was eating breakfast, Patrice goes into the porch to fetch the things she got for everyone, "Mum and grandma can I ask a favour please and can you both shut your eyes and hold your hands out please as I have something very special to give to you both, don't worry it's not a spider or anything."

Once they both had their eyes closed and their hands were out, Patrice gives them a bunch of flowers each. "Ok you can both open your eyes now and I hope you like what I have given you both as its just to say thanks for always being there for me and taking care of me."

Gabbie was the first to open her eyes, "Oh darling they are lovely how did you know, Lilies was my favourite flower?" After Gabbie said that Charlotte then spoke up, "Oh darling you don't have to thank me as is my job to make sure you're ok otherwise I wouldn't be doing my job properly, but I agree with your grandma they are lovely darling, and I love you so much."

Patrice gave her mum and grandma a massive hug and also gave them a kiss on the cheek each, "Dad and Granddad don't worry I haven't forgotten about you two, can do both do the same please and shut your eyes and hold your arms out."

Paul and Andrew did as they were told and once Patrice handed them their lottery tickets each, "Right you can both open your eyes now, sorry I couldn't buy you any booze I am not old enough to get you booze just yet as I am not 18."

Paul and Andrew both looked shocked, "Oh Patrice darling you didn't have to get us anything but thank you so much and like your mum said if we didn't look after you while you were poorly, we wouldn't be doing our jobs right."

After everyone had breakfast, Gabbie and Paul left to go home and they all said goodbye to each other. Patrice said to her parents, "I had fun last night but don't think I can watch another horror film for a while now as I kept on having nightmares all night and I woke up in a hot sweat as well."

After an hour of Charlotte cleaned up in the kitchen after that lovely breakfast that Patrice had cooked Charlotte goes back into the living room and looks at her daughter, "Darling did you want to try and go to school for a few hours today to see how you get on but if not that's fine with me, but you have to go back to school soon as it's coming up to your exams and you need to do some practise in an exam situation as I can't do that for you while you're at home."

Patrice looked at her mum with a sorry face on her, "I know it's coming up to my exams and I do know that I need some more practise, but I am just frightened in going back in case I get bullied again at school."

Charlotte looked at Patrice and then she started to cry, "Oh darling I know you feel like this but it's for the best and I am sure Mr Connel said he would arrange some extra help for you and try and get you some extra time to do you exams."

Patrice went up to her bedroom and started getting ready for school, when she got downstairs Andrew looked at Patrice, "You don't have to go in today if you don't want to your mum is only looking out for you darling but if you want to go in then that's great and I will take you in and have a word with Mr Connel for you as well and explain why you are late."

Patrice got her shoes and coat on and then she nodded to her dad, "Yes please dad I would appreciate it if you had a word with him for me, please as mum is right as I do need some more practise in doing my mocks as they are important."

Andrew went to get his shoes and coat on then he unlocked the car door for Patrice to get in but just before they left Charlotte said, "I think I will come with you as well if you don't mind darling as I need a few words with Mr Connel myself."

Patrice nodded and they all got into the car and drove up to the school, but while Andrew was parking the car, Nicky saw Patrice coming in the main reception area and went and gave her a hug, "Hi Patrice how are you feeling today, it's so good to see you back at school as it's not been the same without you here as I was getting bullied a lot myself."

Patrice gave Nicky a hug back, "Oh wow thanks for them kind words Nicky they mean a lot and sorry you were getting picked on while I was not here hope they were not to mean to you."

Once Charlotte and Patrice sat down outside Mr Connel's office, Andrew came in and joined them, "I am sorry I was not behind you as I had to find another car parking space as the one, I found was a tight squeeze to get into. Does Mr Connel know we are waiting to see him?"

Charlotte nodded at Andrew then within five minutes of Andrew turning up Mr Connel came out of his office, "Morning Mr and Mrs Umar and Patrice hope you're feeling a bit better today. What can I help you all with today?"

Charlotte looked at Mr Connel and smiled, "We have just come in off the off chance to see if it was ok to talk to you about Patrice coming back to school to do some of her mock tests as she needs to do them now and she had agreed this morning to come back to school even though she is a bit nervous about being here because of what happened last time."

Donald looked at everyone with a smile and said, "That's the right attitude to have Patrice and I am so pleased that you decided to come back to school to do some mock exams. Also, Mr and Mrs Umar I have been talking with some teachers, and they have agreed to give Patrice some extra time in the exams and also to keep a close eye on her as well during every lesson and also during the mock exams and future exams."

Patrice was over the moon that she would be getting extra time on her exams but also, she was a bit nervous about doing them, "What if everyone laughs at me if I am still doing the exams when everyone has finished that would mean they will be picking on me more and calling me thick and everything."

Patrice's parents and also the head teacher looked at Patrice, "Don't worry about that, it just means that you would want to take extra time with your exams that's all. Also, I am sure we can figure something out for you."

After they all had a long chat about Patrice coming back to school to do her mock exams, Patrice went to the toilet and when she got back to the head teachers office, she notices the bullies that beat her up last time she was here so she rushed into the office and slammed the door shut, "I am sorry about slamming the door Mr Connel it's just that I saw the bullies who hurt me and put me back in my recovery."

Mr Connel opened the door to see where they were, but they had all gone down to the assembly room to do some mock tests. "It's ok Patrice they have all gone down to the hall to do their mock tests so you shouldn't have to worry about bumping into them. Don't worry I will have a word with all the teaching staff, and I will see what sort of help we can give you and if you want to come back next week and start a new week off at school then you can do as that will also give me time to sort out extra help for you for when you come back."

Andrew and Charlotte gave Donald a handshake, "Thank you so much for seeing us today we appreciate it and thanks for letting Patrice come back next week to start a fresh week and for also to sort out extra help for her as well."

After they all said goodbye to each other they headed down to the car and Andrew says, "Who wants to go to Mcdonalds for something to eat and then I will take my two favourite women in my life shopping as its all on me?"

Charlotte looked at Patrice and then they both looked at Andrew, "Can we afford to do this with the cost of living and all the bills going up?"

Andrew smiled at Charlotte, "Don't you worry about money and just let me treat my two favourite women for once please darling."

Charlotte and Patrice smiled at each other than Andrew drove into the car park at Mcdonalds and went through the drive through and ordered some food for them all.

After they had their Big Mac meals, Andrew gave them £100 each and told them to take as long as they wanted in the shops and to get something nice as he was just going to nip somewhere. "You girls have fun won't you, I will pick up both up in an hour or so I just need to nip to get something."

At this point Charlotte was getting a bit worried, "Darling please tell me the truth where are you getting this sort of money from as we don't have this much ourselves hope you're not getting yourself into any bother or anything."

Andrew looked at Charlotte with a smile on his face, "Don't worry darling I am not in any trouble everyone at work got a huge bonus this year for doing so well and I have been made manager as well with good wages so don't worry, we can afford this."

Once Charlotte got things straight in her mind, her and Patrice went over to the shops and went clothes shopping Patrice even tried on some sexy clothes and while she was showing her mum the clothes that she had on a young lad couldn't keep his eyes of Patrice, so he decided to go over to her, "Excuse me is your name Patrice Umar? I don't know if you remember me, but we used to go to church together and we were in the same home group as each other as well my name is Terry Bloomer?"

Patrice looked at her mother then looked back at Terry, "Oh yes, I remember you now, I had a massive crush on you back in the day, but I never thought you recognised me. Hope your keeping well and how's the family?"

Terry who was pretty tall, over six-foot, blue eyes and a good build replied, "I am doing good thanks and my family are great I have a respectable job now, I just finished my induction course to be a trainee fire fighter. Of course, I recognised you, who wouldn't a good-looking woman like yourself; hope your parents are doing well also?"

Charlotte came over to where Patrice was standing, "Hello Terry how are you doing? How's your family? I can't believe how much you have changed as I remember you being a right little monster and kissing all the girls in Sunday school and back chatting the vicar as well and all the adults."

Terry looked puzzled at Charlotte, "Was I really that bad? I can't remember doing any of that but then again, I was only young, but I have grown up a lot now though. I am just shopping with my parents if you want me to go and fetch them as I know they would love to see you both and to see how you're all doing?"

After five minutes of Terry going to fetch his parents, Patrice quickly went back to the changing room and got changed out of the clothes she was trying on, "Oh mum I can't believe that Terry can remember me as I had a massive crush on him when we went to Sunday School. I think I will buy these clothes as well but only if you like them mum?"

Charlotte smiled at her daughter, "Off course I love the clothes you picked, as you looked like a princess waiting for her prince to come and whisk her off her feet."

After Patrice got changed Terry and his parents came over to where Charlotte and Patrice were in the shop. "Mrs Umar, you remember my mum, and this is my stepdad, Derek, as my dad died a while ago of Cancer, sadly."

Charlotte looked shocked as she never knew that "Hi Madison it's nice to see you after all these years, and I am so sorry to hear about Greg dying he was a lovely chap."

Madison gave them both a hug and a kiss on the cheek each, "It's okay it was a quick death, poor

Greg didn't suffer, this is my new husband, Derek Turnbridge we went to school with each other."

Madison and Charlotte exchanged phone numbers and Terry and Patrice did the same, "Well it was nice to see you again Terry and Madison and it was nice meeting you Greg I don't mean to sound rude, but we are on a time limit as Andrew will be picking us up soon and we still have a lot of shopping to get done before Andrew comes to pick us up."

Madison smiled back, "Yes, I understand that men don't like waiting ages do they for us women, I hope you keep in touch with me though as it would be good for a catch up as it's been years since we have seen each other."

Charlotte smiled back at Madison, "Yes, I agree we do need a girly catch up soon as if I remember rightly, we used to be best mates back in the day? Text or ring me whenever you want to and hope to see you soon look after yourselves."

Just before Patrice followed her mum to the till, she looked at Terry, "I would love to keep in touch with you if that's ok with you unless you have a girlfriend or anything then I will understand and hope to hear from you soon. I better go and follow my mother now look after yourself."

Terry smiled back at Patrice and said the same to her as well.

CHAPTER 20

The next morning, Patrice came skipping down the stairs as she was happy for some reason, something inside was blooming, Charlotte looked at Patrice "Morning sweetheart how are you feeling today? Let me guess what has got you all happy and jolly this morning was it Terry by any chance as not seen you this happy in a while."

Patrice smiled back at her mum, "How did you guess mum, as we were texting each other last night till early hours of this morning and he said he wants to take me out one day as well, but it depends on what you and dad said first."

Andrew couldn't help but hear that his little girl was texting a bloke all night and he wasn't incredibly pleased about it, "What's this I just heard, my little girl fancies a fella, and was texting each other all night what's his name and where is he from? I need words with this bloke."

Patrice started to cry as she didn't want to stop texting Terry, "Dad you don't need to worry about me, and can you remember when I used to go to Sunday school and I kept on going on about this lad called Terry who I had a massive crush on, well me and mum bumped into him and his mum yesterday while we were out shopping and I went bright red when he saw me trying on clothes and showing them to mum and we all got talking and well we all swapped numbers and we were just catching up on old times."

Andrew was a bit puzzled as he was trying to think of who Terry was, "Oh was he the one who was being cheeky to your mum and if I remember rightly also with the vicar?"

Charlotte looked at Andrew with a grin on her face, "Yes darling you got that right, but he's changed a lot and he's even a fire fighter now as well and he's on good money."

Andrew turned back to face his daughter, "In that case message him back and invite him round for tea tonight and I will cook since it's a special occasion."

Patrice got her phone out of her pocket and rang Terry up "Hi Terry, you all, right? I can't believe how long we were texting each other for last night, but just a quick question, are you busy tonight by any chance as my dad has asked me to ask you if you wanted to come round for tea tonight if you have other plans that's fine, just my dad wants to meet you again as told my parents that you want to take me out one night."

Terry sounded shocked as he always thought that Andrew didn't like him, "No I am not busy tonight and I would love to come round for tea what time shall I be there for?"

Patrice whispered that question to her dad while she was still on the phone, "My dad says come round about five as we have tea at six and that will give him an hour to talk to you before tea and he said if you wanted to, we could go out after tea as well for a bit."

After Patrice put the phone down, she went straight over to her dad and gave him a massive hug, "You don't know how much this means to me dad; thank you so much for inviting him round for tea as I still have a massive crush on him."

After an hour of Patrice talking with her parents, she decided to take Shaky out for a bit but only round the block as it was throwing it down with rain. "I am just taking shaky out round the block for a bit as she needs to be let out for a poo but don't worry, I will be okay by myself."

Patrice got her shoes and raincoat on and then she got Shaky on her lead then she headed out the door and went round the block so Shaky could get some air as well as doing a poo.

While she was on the way back home with Shaky she bumped into Terry and she went all red faced again, "Oh hi Terry, what you doing in my neck of the woods as I thought I was seeing you tonight for tea but to be honest I am glad I bumped into you as I am starting to feel a bit dizzy and weak for whatever reason but I think it's because I have not had any breakfast, would you be able to walk with me back home please?"

Terry smiled as he grabbed hold of Shaky's lead and helped to walk Patrice back home, but just before they got to the front gate Patrice went a funny colour and luckily Terry managed to catch her before she fell over. "Patrice, are you ok? We better get you in right away."

When they arrived at the front door, Charlotte caught sight of Terry holding onto Patrice and rushed outside to help bring Shaky and Patrice back in. "Thank you, Terry, for bringing her to the front door as I saw you walking down the street with her from my bedroom window, and I rushed downstairs, and I kept an eye on you both at the door in case you needed my help."

Terry smiled at Charlotte, "You're more than welcome as I was heading to the shop and found Patrice near the shop just going round the corner with Shaky so thought I would stop and see if she was okay as she didn't look too good but then again,

I haven't seen her in ages and I just wanted to make sure she got home safely."

Once they got Patrice in and sat on the sofa, Charlotte turned to Terry, "Did you want to pop in for a cuppa tea as I have just boiled a pot if you wanted one as you look cold, unless you have to get back?"

At this point, Andrew was walking into the living room as he heard all the motion that was happening downstairs as he was getting ready to go for a meeting at work, "What's going on here then? I take it you're the famous Terry, Patrice has been going on about all morning?"

Charlotte looked at her husband, "Darling, do you want a cup of tea before you head out for you meeting as I have just made a pot and I am making Terry one as well as he was kind enough to bring Patrice back home as she was feeling a bit dizzy and weak."

Andrew looked at his watch, "Yes please my darling as I have just got time for one cup then I will have to go to this dreaded meeting which I am not looking forward in going."

After Andrew drank his cup of tea, he said bye to Patrice and Charlotte and headed straight out to his car and then he drove to work even though he was dreading going into work as she still had a lot more deadlines to finish.

After an hour of Terry being round at Patrice's house with her and Charlotte, he looked at them both with a sorry look on his face, "I am sorry to do this, but I really have to go home now as my mum was expecting me back half an hour ago with the shopping. But don't worry I will be back later on. See you both later."

After Terry had gone, Patrice was starting to feel a bit better after a slice of toast and a hot cup of tea, "Oh mum I was so lucky that Terry was walking to the shop when I felt a bit strange cause I don't know what I would have done if I fainted and lost Shaky."

Charlotte gave her daughter a big hug and a kiss, "I know baby girl don't worry your safe now and you're getting a bit of colour back in your cheeks now which is good."

Patrice went to check to see if Shaky was okay and luckily, she was after five minutes of Patrice being back in the living room, her phone made a weird noise and it was a text from Terry, "**Hi Patrice I was just checking in to see how you was feeling now, as you gave me a fright when I found you, I am outside your front door as I have a little surprise for you and I want to take you to my mums for a bit if that's okay as she would like to meet** you again properly and have a cuppa with you but only if you feel up to it."

Patrice screamed and ran straight to the door, but before she managed to open the door Charlotte came rushing to her to see why she was screaming, "Darling is everything all right? I heard you scream."

Patrice showed her mum the text message that Terry had sent her and Charlotte smiled at her and nodded in agreement for her to go round his house for a few hours, "That's fine darling you can go round to his house but promise me one thing you will behave and always use your manners which I know you do anyway but make sure you're back for five as you know what your dad's like."

Patrice hurried and got her shoes and coat on then went outside to meet Terry, "Hi I didn't think we would be seeing each other again till teatime, but this is a delightful surprise. I am feeling a bit better now and my mum says I have got some colour back in my cheeks, which is good."

Terry smiled at Patrice, and he pointed to a lovely blue mini he just bought as he passed his test a few months ago, "Your carriage awaits you and you look lovely today I must admit and yes I agree with your mum you're looking a lot better."

Patrice looked shocked as she didn't know even know that Terry drove a car, "Oh wow this is a beauty when did you get a car and more to the point, I didn't even know you drove."

Terry looked at Patrice and started to laugh, "I have been driving for a while now as don't forget I am nearly nineteen now and my mum bought me this as an early birthday pressie as it was at a bargain price and that is why my mum wanted me back when I left yours but don't worry, I let her know what happened and told her I was on the way when I left yours earlier."

Terry was a proper gentleman with Patrice as he opened the passenger side door for her to get in and then he shut the door when she was belted up and all sorted.

Once Terry got in the car, he put his seatbelt on and off they went to Terry's house and Patrice was a bit nervous about properly meeting his mum and his stepdad again after all these years apart from when she saw them in the shop the other day.

Once they arrived at his house, Terry was the first person out of the car and he was a proper gentleman again and opened the passenger side door for Patrice, "Don't worry my mum and stepdad won't bite you unless they are hungry, no, only kidding but seriously no need to look so frightened after we have had a drink with my mum and stepdad we can go up to my room if you want so we can have some privacy and have a nice chat. While I am being honest, I have to admit that I do fancy you like rotten Patrice."

Patrice went bright red and shocked in a way, "Oh you do fancy me then, as I didn't know if to say anything like that to you, but you already knew that I liked you for a long time but then because I didn't see you for a long time, I forgot about you until we bumped into each other at the shops."

Terry didn't know what to say back to Patrice other then, "I understand what you mean as I was the same as I fancied you back in the day but because we didn't really hang out with each other as I had my own mates and was in that band, "The Pickering's" I spent most of my time doing stuff for the band."

Patrice smiled and they went into Terry's house, but when Patrice got inside a massive a massive Bulldog called Pongo went running straight for her, but Terry made sure Pongo didn't jump up at her.

Patrice took her shoes and coat off and Terry grabbed them from her and hung her coat up and he put her shoes with his in front of the door on the mat.

Madison came to the door and greeted Patrice with a kiss on both cheeks and also the same with Terry, "Please come in both of you as I have just put the kettle on what do you want to drink tea or coffee?"

Patrice smiled at Madison, "Can I have a cup of tea please with two sugars and a little bit of milk."

Madison nodded as she sort of guessed what Terry would pick so she went to make a pot of tea for them all. "Please make yourself at home Patrice and go and take a seat in the living room as I won't be long."

Not long after Patrice went to sit in the living room with Terry and Derek, Madison brought in a tray with a pot of tea and some very old photos of the youth club both Terry and Patrice went to.

Patrice looked shocked as she couldn't remember half of these photos, "Oh wow Mrs Therma, I can't remember any of these pictures at all, but they are lovely though and thanks for the cup of tea."

Madison smiled back and Terry grabbed Patrice's hand and took her up to his bedroom as he wanted to show her how good he was on the drums as she never got to see him play them as she was never allowed out after nine and that was when his group was playing at concerts.

Once they got upstairs, Terry looked at Patrice "I am sorry about dragging you up here like that I just wanted to spend some quality time with you before we go back to yours to have some tea as we have a lot of catching up to do."

Patrice smiled back at Terry, "That's fine but you could of just asked me to follow you without dragging me upstairs as you nearly pulled my arm out of the socket."

Once Terry shut his bedroom door, Patrice sat on the bed while Terry played her a song that he wrote himself called" You mean the world to me, and I can't live without you in my life."

After he played that song to her, she started to cry, "Oh Terry that was lovely I so wish I could have come to see you and your band play years ago I can't believe my parents were so strict with me back in the day."

Terry came to sit on the bed and then all off a sudden, he leaned into Patrice, taking her by surprise and started to kiss her all over which gave her a shock and then she pushed him off her.

After she pushed him off, she regretted it and then she leaned in for a kiss and one thing led to another and they were both under his bed sheets, naked as they were having passionate sex even though Patrice was only sixteen.

After about fifteen minutes, Patrice phone rang and it was her mum, "Hi darling just wondered if you were okay, your dads just called me and he said he's got some good news for us tonight so he wants to take us all out for a posh dinner and he said don't worry, Terry can still come to the restaurant as well and you still have to be back for five."

After Charlotte said what she had to say to her daughter, "Okay mum, don't worry we won't be late, and I am having a fantastic time. Terry has played me one of his songs he wrote ages ago on his drums and he's pretty good as well. I can't believe you and dad didn't let me go to one of his concerts back in the day as there were loads of kids my age, who had gone. Mrs Therma is looking after me really well. Love you loads, mum and see you later."

After she got off the phone with her mum, Terry and Patrice started to kiss lustily and they had passionate sex again; but this time they tried a unique way as it seemed like Patrice was getting a bit sore and a bit anxious as she was only young and inexperienced.

After an hour of them being upstairs Madison shouted, "It's getting near to five now, you two better get ready, Patrice, your mum just text me to say you need to go home now and get ready as your dads on the way home earlier then what he said."

Patrice quickly got dressed and went to the top of the stairs, "Thank you Mrs Therma I forgot what time it was as I was enjoying listening to some of Terry's songs, he used to do years ago, and they are brilliant."

Within five minutes of Patrice talking to Madison, Terry came out of his bedroom door and turned to look at Patrice, "Right we better be going then. I just hope this shirt looks okay on me as I am ever so nervous about going for tea with your parents."

Madison walked halfway up the stairs to where Terry was, "Darling you look like a million dollars don't worry. But just one thing try not to swear in front of Patrice's parents; although I don't mind, they might mind you swearing and here is some money so you can get everyone a drink, so they don't think your being tight as you don't have any cash."

Terry kissed his mum on her cheek, and they headed out to Terry's car, and they went straight to Patrice's house so she could get changed. But while she was getting changed, Terry was having a man-to-man chat with her dad, as Andrew was still not sure about Terry because of how old he was. "Terry, I like you I really do, but I need to make sure you're the right bloke for my little girl and I hope you understand that and if you hurt her and I mean if you really hurt her then I will come and hunt you down and kill you."

Terry was getting a bit scared now, "Mr Umar, please don't worry I will never hurt your daughter as I think I am starting to fall in love with her again and I love spending time with her as she is dead pretty and funny and I am just surprised no one has grabbed her by now."

Patrice started to walk down the stairs with a lovely light blue dress which reached to the floor, and she had a pair of Irregular choice shoes on which were called Ban Joes and they were dead sparkly and black with a little bow on the top.

Patrice's parents and also Terry couldn't believe how lovely Patrice looked in her blue dress, "Oh darling you look so lovely, but I can't remember you picking this out at the shops when we went shopping."

Patrice looked at her mum, "I sneaked it in the shopping trolley when you were not looking as I didn't think you would let me buy it. I wanted to try something new for a change as I want to be more popular with the other kids at school."

Terry was so speechless as to what to say other then, "Oh Patrice you looked lovely and that really suits you and don't worry what anyone else says about you as you're so kind it's unreal; and that is what made you stand out years ago."

Andrew smiled at Terry as he knew he got his thoughts and feelings wrong about Terry, "I agree with your mum and Terry, never let anyone bully you into wearing what you're not used to wearing and do me one favour sweetheart never change who you are please."

Patrice started to cry with all the nice comments everyone gave her, then they headed out to Andrew's car so they could go to the restaurant for a nice meal to celebrate Andrew's news.

Once they all got in the restaurant called "Yonga" Terry and Patrice went to ask someone if there was a table free for four people and if there was a window seat as well. "Excuse me Sir we were wondering if there is a free table for 4, possibly, please near a window?"

The waiter looked in his book, "You're lucky someone has not long cancelled their table for tonight and it's near the window; and it's also got a lovely view as well. I will take you over if you can follow me, please."

Patrice and Terry started to follow the waiter until Patrice started to have a meltdown as she saw someone she didn't want to see after what had happened before, when she had run off during the first meeting with her head teacher and got beat up.

Terry looked shocked as to why she was having a meltdown, "Patrice, are you okay? What's up?"

Patrice wiped the tears off her face, "I will be okay once we get to our table and my parents are with us, I have just seen someone I don't like and never want to see again."

They quickly sat down at the table, when Charlotte and Andrew came over with the drinks, "I have got us all a bottle of wine to share each, and don't worry Patrice I have asked the bar staff if you will be allowed a glass as your only 16 and your allowed alcohol while you're with your parents but of cause you can't order it when you're not with us, deal?"

Patrice nodded and then Andrew started to pour everyone a glass of Chardonnay, "Right I bet your all wondering why I have brought us all here today, well I have some news to tell you all, I have been made a partner in the business, which will mean I can sometimes work from home, and it will mean more money coming in. I also have a business credit card so for this meal it's from the company as they have paid for this."

Charlotte and Patrice gave Andrew a big hug, "Well done darling that's wonderful news." "Yeah, dad I am so pleased for you that's great."

Terry didn't know what to say apart from, "I am so pleased for you Mr Umar but please let me buy us all a drink after this one to celebrate."

After Andrew gave his speech, the waiter came over, "Are you all ready to order?"

Charlotte looked at the menu repeatedly, "Yes, can I have the beef stew, please." Everyone else looked at the menu and they didn't know what to order so

Patrice and Terry replied, "Can we have the lasagne please with a side of chips." Then Andrew replied, "Can I just order the hot pot please?"

The waiter nodded and then he went over to the till and placed everyone's order.

After an hour of them all waiting for their meals, the waiter came back with their meals, and they started to eat. While they were eating Patrice was trying to play footsy with Terry but instead, she was doing it with her dad who also thought that Charlotte was doing that to him.

After everyone had finished, Terry checked his phone and he saw that his mum text him to ask Patrice and her family over for a cup of coffee, "Sorry to disturb you all, but I have just had a text off mum, who has asked me to ask you all over for a cuppa or anything else if you fancy and we have plenty of room if you would want to stay over if you fancied some beer or wine."

Andrew and Charlotte looked at each other, "We would love that, yes please as it would give me and your mum and stepdad a chance to have a catch up."

Terry decided to ring his mum instead of texting her, "Hi mum just me, I have just asked them for you, and they all agreed to pop over and I said if they fancied something stronger that we have enough space if they wanted to stay over hope that's cool."

Madison sounded a bit shocked as she sort of knew why he suggested that "Yes that fine with me as it would be good to have a catch up with them properly."

Everyone got in Andrew's car and drove round the corner to where Terry and his family lived. Once everyone got out of the car, Terry went straight to his front door and opened it up for everyone to run inside as it was chucking it down now and they didn't want to get wet.

Madison took everyone's coats from them and put them in the conservatory and hung them up on coat hangers so they would dry just in case they didn't want to stay over.

Everyone was having such a laugh as they were playing loads of games but the best one that they played was Pictionary which was men vs women and the women won as they were better drawers.

It was getting late, and everyone was falling asleep, Madison especially was falling asleep, "Right I am going up to bed now as I am falling asleep do you all want to stay over as I don't want you driving back in the dark and especially because we have had a lot to drink. Night everyone."

Andrew, Charlotte, and Patrice all nodded, "Oh yes please if that's okay with you."

Madison nodded and she went to get the spare rooms already for them to go to bed, "Would you all be fine in one room, or I can bring a quilt down for someone to sleep on the sofa as if I am honest, I don't fancy Patrice or Terry sleeping in the same bed, really, because you never know what they would get up to."

Charlotte and Andrew smiled as they felt the same, "I agree with you as they are still young, and we can sort something out as we can manage to sleep in the same bedroom if that will be easier for you."

Patrice looked at her parents with a very weird look, "I will sleep on the sofa and my parents can have the bed as I can sleep anywhere, and it will be a bit weird me sleeping in the same room as my parents."

CHAPTER 21

Early in the morning, Terry woke up as he fancied a glass of milk as he couldn't sleep as he knew that Patrice was downstairs and all he could think about was being next to her.

So, he got up and sneaking as quietly as he could down the stair, he tried to get under the quilt with Patrice, "Are you awake my darling sexy Patrice? As I can't sleep knowing you're down here all by yourself and I am in my bed."

Patrice opened her eyes quickly, "What you doing down here?" Blurry eyed, she could just make out the clock in the dim light. "It's so early but, I so wish I could have slept next to you in your nice warm bed as I keep hearing noises in your house, and I am so scared."

Terry looked puzzled as the number of times he slept on the sofa when he arrived home late at night, and he didn't want to wake his parents up he never heard any noises. "Oh Patrice, I have come to give you a hug and to try and sneak under the quilt and cuddle up with you and other things but I know we can't, unless we are very quiet and I can sleep next to you for a few hours, but then I will have to sneak back up to my room before everyone else wakes up so they don't expect a thing, but we will have to set the alarm on my phone for 7 so I can quickly go back up to my room, so no one expects a thing."

Patrice pulled the quilt up so Terry could snuggle up to her on the sofa and then one thing led to another, and they were getting into a bit of four play, which led to them having sex on the sofa.

After an hour of them having a bit of fun, they fell asleep and then Terry's phone alarm went off so he rushed as quietly as he could back up to his room, so no one knew he sneaked to sleep next to Patrice.

While Terry was sneaking back upstairs, Derek came out of his bedroom while Terry was coming back up as Derek needed the loo, "Don't worry son, I won't tell your mum or Patrice's parents what you were doing as I was like you when I was young and one of my girlfriends stayed over at mine one night on my parent's sofa as I so wanted my girlfriend at the time to sleep in my bed but my parents were old school as well. So, your secret is safe with me."

Terry smiled at his stepdad and went back in his bedroom and made out to his mum when she woke up that he stayed in his room all night.

When it got to 8am, Charlotte quickly jumped out of her skin as she heard a noise from inside the house and she was scared, "Andrew did you hear that it sounded like it came from downstairs, and I sure hope that it was not Patrice and she fell off the sofa as she is not used to sleeping on the sofa."

Andrew quickly woke up and rushed to get dressed and went to check to see if Patrice was okay, but when he got downstairs, he saw Derek, "Morning mate how are you feeling this morning? Charlotte nearly jumped out of her skin as she thought Patrice had fallen off your sofa and banged her head or something."

Derek turned around to face Andrew, "Oh sorry I didn't mean to wake you, I was trying to be as quiet as I could as I need to go to work soon and I was just making Madison some breakfast as I am going to Cuba on a work trip and I won't see her for a week; do you want me to make you lot some breakfast while I am doing some for Madison as well?"

Andrew shook Greg's hand and nodded his head, "Yes please mate that would be perfect then we will get out of your hair I will just go and wake Patrice up and let her and Charlotte know."

While he was waking Patrice up, Charlotte came down the stairs as she was wondering what was going on as Andrew was taking ages and she thought Patrice had hurt herself. "Is everything okay darling as I was starting to get worried as you didn't come straight back up to me and let me know."

Andrew gave Charlotte a smile, "Yes don't worry, Patrice is fine, she was still fast asleep, and it was just Derek in the kitchen making Madison some breakfast and he said he will make us lot some as well."

Charlotte went into the kitchen and went to see Derek, "I just wanted to thank you for doing us all some breakfast that's so kind of you and just want to thank you again for letting us stay the night."

Derek turned round as he was just stirring the beans as he was making a full English breakfast for everyone, "You're more than welcome as it was a pleasure, and I had a good time as well."

After Charlotte spoke with Derek, she made her way into the living room to check up on Patrice, "Morning darling did you manage to sleep well on the sofa as your dad said to me last night when we got to bed that you could have had the bed with me, and he would have slept on the sofa."

Patrice looked at her mum with a big fat smile, "I slept like a log thanks for asking mum. Did I hear Derek say he was making a full English breakfast for us all?"

Charlotte smiled and nodded at her daughter then she went back upstairs to make the bed that her, and Andrew slept in.

After half an hour of Charlotte making up the bed, Madison and Terry came downstairs and Terry gave Patrice a smile and kissed her on the cheek, "Morning Patrice hope you slept okay on the sofa as I know it's not comfy sleeping on that thing. I never thought I could have slept on the sofa, and you could have had my bed."

Patrice smiled at Terry, "I slept like a log thank you and I would have said no as that's your bed and that wouldn't have been right to take your bed from you."

Terry smiled at Patrice and they both went into the kitchen to get some breakfast. While everyone was eating, Derek took Madison her breakfast up to her in bed so he could spend some time with her before he left for Cuba for a week. "Morning Darling you, ok? Did you have a nice lie in this morning? I thought I would bring you breakfast in bed for a change, and I can spend some quality time with you before I have to go to Cuba for work."

Madison turned around and looked at Derek, "Oh morning darling, I never heard you get up I must have been fast asleep. That looks yummy, but if I am honest, I am not hungry for that, yet I am starving for something else if you know what I mean."

Derek couldn't put the tray down quick enough, and he also checked his watch to see if he had time, "You're in luck you sexy mama I have two hours to spare before my taxi arrives, but we will have to be quiet as don't forget we have quests."

Madison went to lock their bedroom door and then she jumped on Derek, and they started to undress each other and did unthinkable things to each other, but Madison had to put a sock in her mouth, so no one heard her scream or even make noises."

After Charlotte, Andrew, Patrice, and Terry all had breakfast they all left to go their separate ways and Terry shouts to his parents, "We are all off now you two and they all say thanks for a good night and Charlotte will text you during the week mum to invite us round to theirs to repay the favour."

Once everyone had left, Madison felt awful as she didn't say goodbye to Charlotte, Andrew, Terry, or Patrice so she quickly got up and went to search for her phone, "Hi Charlotte I just wanted to say sorry I wasn't downstairs to say goodbye to you before you left, it's just that Derek brought me breakfast in bed as I didn't have a good night and also Derek just wanted to spend some time with me as he's going to Cuba for a week as it's for work. Let me make it up to you lot please?"

Charlotte looked at Andrew and Patrice with a big fat smirk on her face, "It's ok Madison don't worry we understand you don't have to explain yourself to me as me and Andrew know what it's like when your other half is going away on a business trip, and you just want to spend some time with each other before the other person goes away."

When Charlotte, Andrew and Patrice got home, they all went to sit on the sofa and made a right fuss of Shaky as it was a while since she was left by herself, "Oh Shaky we are so sorry we left you all night we are bad but it's time for walkies now."

Shaky was getting so excited and started to jump up Charlotte, but when Charlotte went to find the lead, she found a note on the table near her lead which read "**Hi darling, me and your mum popped by last night to see if you were all ok and to see what happened at the school and we didn't see your car so we let ourselves in and found that Shaky had wet the floor so we took her for a walk around the bloke and we cleaned the floor for you as well. Love mum and dad.**"

Charlotte couldn't believe that Shaky did that, but she wasn't mad or anything. So, she gets her mobile out and rings her dad up, "Hi dad, thanks for coming round last night, and sorry we were not in, you could have phoned us as we decided to stay round a mates last night who we knew years ago from church, and we all had a good old catch up with each other. Also, thanks for coming in and checking on Shaky for us and also for cleaning up her mess give our love to mum for us please and we love you too."

After Charlotte got off the phone, she grabs Shakey's lead and took her round the block for a little walk and a little play with her on the park then they came home.

It was getting near to teatime now, and neither Charlotte nor Andrew could be bothered to cook so they ordered a pizza for them all and they all sat on the sofa eating and having a laugh with each other.

CHAPTER 22

The next morning, Patrice got up before her parents as she wanted to make herself a pack lunch ready for school. She thought it was best to go to school so she can get back to normal. "Mum, Dad, I have made you both some toast for breakfast and I am going to go into school today as I need to get on with doing some more mock exams and to get back to normality, so I am just off to go and get the school bus, see you both later."

Just when Charlotte was coming out of her bedroom to shout to Patrice it was too late as she had already left to go and catch the bus, so she decided to ring her, "Darling are you sure about going into school today? If you get worried or anything or you don't feel well ring me or your dad and we will come and fetch you straight away. We both love you so much and think you're a brave lady doing this."

Once Patrice got to school, she went straight to Mr Connel's office to let him know that she decided to come back so she can get back to normal and to see if she had been granted some extra time to do her exams. "Hi Mr Connel, just to let you know that I have decided to come back to school, and I was wondering if you managed to sort anything out for me to help me with everything? Also is the school nurse in today as I really need to talk to her, please?"

Mr Connel looked shocked as he didn't expect Patrice to come back just yet, "Oh hello Patrice nice to see you back, yes, the nurse is in, but she is just seeing another pupil at the minute but feel free to wait outside her room if you want to. Also, yes, I have managed to sort everything out for you, and Mrs Bourbon is expecting you as she is going to be helping you from now on."

Patrice smiled at Mr Connel then she went to wait outside the nurse's office as she really needed to see the nurse.

After five minutes of Patrice waiting outside the nurse's office, another pupil came out of the office crying then the nurse said, "Hi Patrice, how are you feeling as I heard what happened to you? What can I do for you today my dear?"

Patrice went all quiet as she didn't know where to start, "Well thanks for seeing me on this short notice, I am a bit worried as I have not had my period yet and I am worried. I can't talk to my parents about it as then they will know I have slept with someone as they don't believe in that sort of thing. Is there anything you can do to help me please?" Patrice blabbered out nervously.

The nurse, Norma, replied with a slight smile on her face, "I think there is something I can do as I am going to a place in Nottingham where they do all sort of tests to see if women are pregnant as I can't do that sort of thing in school. I am afraid but we will have to get authority from Mr Connel to see if I can take you out of school for a few hours if that's suitable for you and hopefully to put your mind at rest?"

Patrice smiled at Norma, "Thank so you much that would be perfect, and I didn't really want to come back to school today but I had to get checked out without my parents knowing. Also, would you have to let my parents know where I am as I don't want them knowing?"

Norma smiled at Patrice, "I understand don't worry dear as that is why I am here to help girls in your situation, who feel like they can't talk to either of their parents. I will just go and have a word with Mr Connel for you, if you can just sit here for a little while please?"

Patrice smiled at Norma then she went to see Mr Connel, "Sorry to bother you Mr Connel, I was just wondering if I can get your permission to take Patrice out of school for a few hours please; as this situation can't be dealt with here, I am afraid and I will bring her straight back after."

Mr Connel turned around in his chair as he was looking out of the window at something, "If the situation can't be dealt with in school and you have to take her out then that is what you have to do. I will sort the paperwork out when you get back."

Norma smiled at Mr Connel, "Thank you so much sir, also Patrice is worried in case her parents ring up to see how she is, and she was wondering if you would lie and just say that she's gone out on a field trip with a class. I know you don't like lying but Patrice is so scared in case her parents find out where she is."

Mr Connel nodded in agreement as he didn't want to upset Patrice and make her any worse, "Okay I will lie to her parents but only this time as I don't want to stress Patrice out and make her feel worse that she can't come back to school and that she can't trust me either."

Norma smiled and went back to her office to let Patrice know the good news, "I have some good news for you Patrice, Mr Connel has agreed to lie to your parents if they ring to check up on you but only this once as he don't want to stress you out and make you not trust him again."

Patrice went over to Norma and gave her a massive hug, "Thank you so much I appreciate it. When can we leave?"

Norma started to get her coat on, "We can go now if you want to, but I will just need to ring them first to let them know I am bringing you down with me to get some tests done."

Just before they were about to leave, Mr Connel came into the nurse's room, "I have just been thinking, as you can never tell how long these things can last can you, so I was thinking, if I give you some money, Norma, you can take Patrice somewhere of her choice then it is like a field trip isn't it and then I won't be lying to her parents if they ring up?"

Patrice didn't know what to say to Mr Connel, "Thank you so much sir you don't know how much this means to me, and I just hope no one in school will find out about this, as I don't want any more reason for them to pick on me."

Once Mr Connel gave Norma some cash, they both headed to her car so they can go to Nottingham so Patrice can put her mind at rest. While they were in the car, Norma put the radio on to try and relax Patrice a bit as she could tell she was anxious going to get some tests done without letting her parents know as she never lies to her parents, but she had to on this one occasion.

When they got to Nottingham and got to the sexual health clinic, they had to go up two flights of stairs to where Patrice had to go. Norma looked at Patrice, "If you go and take a seat for me, I will go and get you checked in and have a word with one of my colleagues and explain the situation as I am sure they will see you."

Patrice did as she was told, and within ten minutes of her sitting down Norma shouted her over and they went into a private room with another nurse. "Hello Patrice, my name is Sandra, and I will be helping you today can you tell me a bit about what the problem is please?"

Patrice started to cry, and Norma went over to where she was sitting and held her hand, "It's okay, you don't have to feel nervous here as I won't leave you, do you want me to tell Sandra what the problem is?"

Patrice nodded and then Norma started to tell Sandra what the problem was. "Patrice has had unprotected sex with a young man she hasn't seen in years, and they have only just got back in touch with each other and now she's worried because she has not had a period."

Norma looked at Patrice to make sure what they had discussed before was accurate, Patrice nodded, "Oh lovely I am sorry to hear that, are you normally on time each month? Well, we can start off by doing some sexual transmitted tests to see if you have caught anything and also do a pregnancy test at the same time if that's okay with you?" Sandra queried.

Patrice nodded and signed a few pieces of paper that gave them permission to do this, and Norma gave her a bottle to go and wee in so they could see if she was pregnant.

Once Patrice got given the bottle to go and do her business in, she headed to the toilet, but she was a bit shaky as well and on quite a few occasions she nearly fell over as she felt so weak.

After Patrice did the wee sample for the nurse, she headed straight back to the room where Norma and Sandra were waiting for her, "I couldn't wee much I'm afraid, but I managed to do a little bit and hope that will be enough for you to test to see if I am pregnant or anything."

Sandra smiled at Patrice and went to dip the wee stick in the appropriate bottle to do the tests she had to do. "If you want to take a seat outside in the waiting area for me, please, Patrice while I have a quick word with Norma and then we will shout you in."

Patrice did as she was asked and went to sit in the waiting area, when suddenly, she noticed this tall looking fella who she was kissing in the woods ages ago when her dad caught her in there, so she quickly covered her face with a magazine, so he didn't recognize her.

Luckily, he didn't recognize her, and he walked straight past her and into a different room.

Within five minutes of Patrice waiting in the waiting area, Norma came back out and asked her to come in, "Patrice can you follow me back into the nurses room."

Once they were all sat down in the nurse's room, Sandra looked at Patrice with a stern look on her face, "I am pleased to tell you that you're not pregnant but I am sorry to say that you have a sexual transmitted disease but don't worry we can give you some tablets to clear it up but it does mean that you will have to tell everyone who you have slept with that you have got this."

Patrice started to cry, "I can't have a disease as the bloke who I thought I was pregnant with was very careful, but then again there was a bloke who I was with a little while ago in the school bushes and we had a quick fool around as I were upset...that was before my dad caught us, and he is here in the clinic but I don't know his name or his number as he was just a lad who was sitting in the bushes hiding from someone the same day I was."

Sandra looked shocked, "Well in this case you can't let him know can you if you don't know who he was or anything and are you sure the last bloke you slept with wasn't using protection or was as that can't always be 100%"

Just as Patrice was looking outside the nurse's room into the waiting area, she spotted that lad who she had a quicky with in the bushes, "Norma he is sat outside in the waiting area now, he's wearing black joggers and a light blue t-shirt with a basketball hat on as well."

Once Patrice pointed him out to her, she went over to him and says, "Excuse me sir, but can I have a quiet word with you a minute please in my office as I don't think you would want me to say this out loud."

The lad looked puzzled, but he did what he was asked, "Sorry to sound rude but why did you want a quiet word with me for, in your office?"

Once Norma shut the door, he then noticed that Patrice was sitting in the corner of the room, "Oh hi again, sorry I can't remember your name, but I never forgot your face as you're so sexy and I was hoping to bump into you again."

Patrice looked shocked because of what he said, "I am sorry to have to do this and to say this, but you need to get tested for a sexually transmitted disease as I have tested positive for one and I need to let everyone know who I slept with/ had fun with so they can get tested."

The young lad looked shocked, "I am sure I never came inside of you but then again, I wouldn't have known if I did as I was a virgin before I saw you in the woods and we had some fun. So yes, I will defo get a test done and will I know the results today as I am seeing a new woman now and if I have got it, I will have to let her know."

Norma looked puzzled, "Well if you were a virgin how would you know how to have sex or anything then? I think you're lying somehow but I can't put my finger on it because while Patrice was telling you the shocking news, you didn't look shocked or anything, so I think you knew you had something in the first place."

The lad called Norman said, "Yes alright then, I knew I had a sexual transmitted disease, and I also knew Patrice before I saw her in the woods as I sort of got paid to get off with her as no one likes her at all."

When Patrice heard this, she ran out of the nurse's room as fast as she could, and Norma ran after her and managed to catch up with her before she ran out of the building. "Oh, Patrice I am so sorry you had to hear that from that nasty piece of a human being just ignore him as your kind, lovely and beautiful and you always make sure everyone else is okay before you are."

Patrice started to calm down a bit, and they both went back up to Sandra's office where Norman and

Sandra were waiting patiently for his results. "Right Norman your results have come back, and you passed the sexual transmitted disease over to Patrice; which means you will both need to go on some tablets to clear it then to come back in a week to just get checked again."

Norman and Patrice didn't want to be in the same room as each other, so when they heard what they did Norman stomped straight out of the room and went to find his girlfriend.

Norma looked at Patrice, "Now we know you're not pregnant, but you have an infection, we will go and fetch your tablets and then we will do whatever you want to do since Mr Connel has given us £100 to spend."

Patrice had a sorry look on her face but also, she was relieved that she was not pregnant as she was too young to get pregnant and her parents wouldn't have been incredibly happy with her either. "To be honest Norma, I am starving as I forgot to bring my lunch bag with me which is still at school. To be fair I would love to do anything, but you can choose since you have been so good and helpful today."

Norma looked at Patrice with a smile, "Well that's my job but I have to admit it I am also hungry so shall we go to burger king and get some food then if you want to, we can go and have a look around the caves of Nottingham if you want and learn about the history of them?"

Patrice smiled and they went to go and have some dinner then to go to the caves of Nottingham to learn about the history of the caves so that they were not wasting Mr Connel's money on anything stupid and also Patrice was also learning so it wasn't a useless day after all.

It was getting near to 2pm now, and Norma and Patrice looked at each other, "I think we better go back to school now don't you Patrice and let Mr Connel know what we have been doing and then you can catch the school bus back home then your parents will never know where you have been."

Patrice smiled at Norma, and they headed back to school, and they headed straight up to Mr Connel's room and gave him the money back what was left over.

When they got back to school, Norma parked her car and Patrice headed straight to Mr Connels office and waited in there till the nurse came to the office as she had the cash, "Oh hello you two did you get everything sorted Patrice and did you have a nice day with Norma?"

Patrice smiled, "Yes thank you, we had a good day thank you for the money as after I did what I had to do we went to the caves of Nottingham, and I learnt the history of why they used the caves which was really fascinating so thank you so much for that Sir."

While Patrice was still in the office, Norma came in and they all had a lovely chat as there was no point Patrice going to her last class as she already missed a day's education, "Just before you go Patrice, your mum rang up the school to see how you were getting on and I said you were out on a visit which was Educational and she was glad that you were getting on fine."

Patrice smiled and she was glad that Mr Connel told her that as it was not a lie as they did some something educational while she was in Nottingham.

It was now time to get the school bus, so she said goodbye to Mr Connel and also thanked Norma for all the help she had given her that day and picked her lunch bag up from her office as well and then she walked down to get the bus to go home.

CHAPTER 23

The next morning, Patrice didn't feel too good, while she was going down the stairs to go to the kitchen to get a cup of tea, she felt a bit sick, so she had to rush back to the bathroom and turn the taps on, so her parents didn't hear her being sick; luckily, she wasn't sick.

When she came out of the bathroom her mum came out of her bedroom, "Morning sweetheart how are you today, Mr Connel told me yesterday you went out to the caves did you have fun darling?"

Patrice looked at her mum with a sorry look on her "I did, yes thanks, mum. But don't think I can go into school today as I think I went back too quickly and think I need a few more days off if that's okay with you and dad?"

Charlotte walked towards her daughter to give her a hug and a morning kiss, "Of course darling as we don't want you fall ill again as you do look a bit pale today. So, I agree, we will keep you off for a few more days just to keep an eye on you."

Andrew was getting up now anyway as he had to go to work, "Morning my two most beautiful ladies in my life how are you both today?"

Charlotte looked at her husband with a smirk on her face as he knew how she was that morning, "I am okay thanks darling even though you were already awake when I got up to go to the bathroom."

Patrice didn't want to know what her mother meant, "I am okay thanks dad apart from I think I pushed myself too quick in going to school yesterday as I don't feel too good now, so I am having a few days off."

While Patrice was talking to her dad, Charlotte got straight onto the phone and rang Mr Connel up, "Sorry to ring you up this early, but I just wanted to let you know that Patrice won't be coming into school for a few days now as she isn't very well hope that's okay with you."

Mr Connel thought that this might happen, "Of course that's fine and don't worry about ringing up at this time either as I am always the first into school as I have to get everything ready for the day ahead."

After Charlotte got off the phone with Mr Connel, she turned to face her daughter, "Right darling, Mr Connel has said that's okay about you not going into school for a few days, but don't worry if you need more time off school that's fine; but you will have to go in eventually. But I am hoping you will be fine to go back in a few days."

Patrice smiled at her mum as she was so glad that she had a few more days off school, "Thanks mum you're a star and I appreciate it. Don't worry if you and dad have to go to work as I will be okay by myself as I have Shaky for company and if I need you or dad, I will call either one of you so please both of you go to work as I am going to crack on with a few things and I might ring Mr Connel up myself to bring me some mock papers round as well so I can get on with the exams."

Charlotte made them all some breakfast before her and Andrew had to dash out to work, but before she went out, she left the number for Mr Connel on the side for Patrice.

After everyone had their breakfast, and Charlotte was heading out the door she shouted to Patrice, "Darling I have left Mr Connel's number on the side for you to ring him for some practise exams and I am so pleased with you for wanting to get on with doing some practise papers"

Not long after Charlotte had left, Andrew was on his way out as well and he gave his daughter a kiss on the cheek, "I know your mum has already said this to you darling, but we are so proud of you wanting to do some practise tests at home but if Mr Connel says he needs to supervise you then invite him to come in and help you or whatever it takes to help you pass the exams."

Patrice smiled at her dad and gave him a kiss on the cheek just before he headed out of the door, "Have a good day dad love you lots, and don't worry I will get in touch with my head teacher in a bit I am just going to watch a bit of TV first."

After an hour of both her parents leaving for work, she gets the house phone and rang Mr Connel, "Sorry to bother you sir its Patrice Umar, I was just wondering if you are not too busy, if you could bring me some practise papers so I can do some more practising, but my dad has said if you need to watch over me doing them while at home then you can do."

Mr Connel sounded shocked at what Patrice just asked him, "Okay Patrice, I can bring you some papers round later this afternoon and yes I can stay for a bit while you do the exam paper, and we can mark them together and see if I can help you in any other way as I don't want you falling behind."

Once Patrice got off the phone with her head teacher, she sat down on the sofa and decided to make an account on Facebook so she can make some friends and meet people who are like her because she was sick of being a loner all the time and not having any mates to go out with or anything.

After she made an account on the computer, she blocked everyone who she knew from school so they wouldn't pick on her on Facebook as well as being picked on at school and she found a few people that she liked and so she decided to add them as a mate and now it was just a waiting game to see if anyone accepts her.

When she logged off on the computer, she decided to get her iPhone 8 out and she went on the app store, downloaded Facebook, and logged in on her phone so she will know when someone accepts her or even sends her a message.

Patrice thought she better let her parents know that she has set up an account before they hear it from someone else, so she sends a text to her parents,

"**Hi, just to let you know that I have set up an account on Facebook and I hope you won't be mad with me, as I am sick of being a loner all the time and not having any mates to go out with, so I thought I would log onto here as everyone at** school is talking about it, even Terry told me about this the other day."

After Patrice sent the text to her parents, she went to make herself a cup of tea as she couldn't stop yawning and she didn't want to have an energy drink all the time as her granddad told her ages ago that if she carried on having energy drinks it would damage her and they are full of sugar and that having a cup of tea would be better.

Within 5 minutes of making a cup of tea, she received a text from her parents, "That's okay with us darling, but just be careful please as there are some weird people on there and we are on there as well and some of your family are as well."

She was so relieved that her parents agreed to her being on there, so she logs back on to her account and does a search for her family members and she finds her parents on there who she adds straight away and then she goes searching for different groups that she might be able to join.

After she spent about an hour finding people on Facebook and trying to make new friends, Mr Connel turned up and knocked on the front door, Patrice jumped up as she didn't realise what time it was as she was to engrossed with Facebook and she ran to the door, "Afternoon sir, thanks for bringing some practise papers round for me to have a go at. Do you want a cup of tea or anything?"

Mr Connel looked at his watch, "I only have a few hours spare for you today Patrice as we really need to get on with some practise papers as it's your exams in a few weeks and starting next week you will have to come back to school as everyone will be doing the proper exams by then. Also, can I have a cup of coffee please, 2 sugars with no milk, thanks."

After she made Mr Connel and herself a drink, they went into the living room and sat at the table to do some practise exams and Mr Connel made sure there was complete silence and even took her mobile off her while she was doing the exam.

Mr Connel looked at his watch, "Right you have an hour to do this paper and I will be sitting on the sofa catching up with some emails as I have brought my work laptop with me, and can I have your mobile as well please as I am going to treat this like a proper exam."

Patrice handed her mobile to Mr Connel as she knows she won't be allowed her mobile in the exam and she was quite pleased that he was treating this like a proper exam, "Yes, here you go Sir, I just hope my parents don't ring me during the exam unless you want to ring my mum up and explain everything to her, so she don't worry?"

Mr Connel nodded his head, "Right Patrice it is now 1pm and you have an hour, good luck and if you have any question just raise your hand and I will come and help you the best I can but I can't give you the answers but I can help you to try and understand them and I will let your mum know as well for you."

Patrice had a slow start as she couldn't remember doing some of the questions that was on the paper, but after 15 minutes of her looking at the exam paper she managed to get in the swing of things. Mr Connel looked at his watch, "Right Patrice you have 30 minutes left to complete the paper."

After her hour was up, Mr Connel said, "Right Patrice your time is up can you put your pen down for me please and close the paper and I will come over and check it with you."

Patrice looked at Mr Connel, "Sir I have not finished the paper and thought I had extra time to complete the exam?"

Mr Connel checked his notes and read all the emails from the exam board, "I did ask that question for you Patrice, but in the real exam they won't allow you to have extra time I am afraid unless you're in a different room from everyone else but I thought you would prefer to be in the same room as everyone so you don't get picked on more; as I am only thinking of you."

Patrice smiled at Mr Connel, "I do understand if I am being honest, I would prefer not to be in a different room to other people as that would make them pick on me more so thank you for understanding, I just hope I pass this exam."

Mr Connel came and sat next to her, "Right I have another paper for you to have a go at this time and it's for maths, while you're doing your maths exam, I will check your English and mark it for you?"

Patrice nodded and then she had a go at her maths exam and the same rules applied to her what she had for her English. Halfway through her doing her maths Mr Connel looked at Patrice, "Right Patrice you have 30 minutes left to complete this paper."

Patrice nodded and got cracking with doing her maths exam even though her eyes kept on closing as she was finding the exams really hard, and she couldn't concentrate properly either for some reason.

After 30 minutes was up for Patrice, Mr Connel looked at Patrice, "Right can you put you pen down please and pass me the paper and I will hand you your mobile again after we have gone through the papers together."

While they were going through her English mock exam, Mr Connel was so pleased on how far Patrice had come on her English, "Right Patrice I have some good news for you, you have passed your mock English with flying colours as I was looking over that while you were doing your maths exam, so let's go through your maths together now."

But before Patrice sat down, she looked at Mr Connel's cup, "Do you want another cup of coffee sir? As if it is okay with you; would you mind me making myself another cup of tea, please, as mine has gone cold as I wasn't sure if I was allowed to drink my tea while I was doing my exams?"

Mr Connel looked in his cup and he forgot he drank it all, "Oh that would be lovely thank you Patrice you're so very kind and thoughtful and of course you were allowed to drink your cup of tea as you're at home but during the exam at school you're not allowed to drink anything."

Patrice went into the kitchen and put the kettle on, but while she was doing that, she heard her phone ringing so she went back into the living, "Sir am I ok to have my phone back please as I think my mum might be calling me as I can hear my phone ringing?"

Mr Connel handed back her phone, "Hi mum everything okay? Sorry I didn't reply to your text, Mr Connel is here, and we have just done some practise exams and guess what, I have passed my English but that's only a mock one though."

While she was on the phone to her mum, Mr Connel noticed that he had an email from the examination board regarding Patrice and her having extra time, "**Dear Mr Connel, I have had another look into Patrice's medical problems and I know I told you that she couldn't have extra time but since I have been non-stop looking into this case I can now confirm that she can have extra time, but I will leave it in your capable hands on how you want to proceed with how you want to do this with her. Kind Regards Examination body.**"

After Patrice got off the phone to her mum, she went into the kitchen and poured herself and Mr Connel some hot water in her cup of tea and in his coffee.

Once Patrice arrived back into the living with both the cups, Mr Connel looked at Patrice with a smile on his face, "You will never believe this Patrice, you know I was telling you that the examination body said you couldn't have extra time, now they are saying you can have extra time, but they are leaving it in my hands on how I can go ahead with doing this."

Patrice couldn't believe what she just heard, "Oh wow thank you so much Mr Connel that has made my day as you saw, I do need extra time. I was struggling doing the exams today, and I will leave it with you on how we progress on giving me extra time. Oh, by the way here's your cup of coffee."

Mr Connel smiled at Patrice and drank his drink as fast as he could as he had to get back to school as it was getting near to the afternoon assembly for everyone; and for him to let everyone know who's doing the exams next week, and the rules and the times of the exams. "Right Patrice thank you so much for the lovely cups of coffee, but I am afraid I have to go back to school now and let everyone know about the exams next week."

After Mr Connel left to go back to school, Patrice got straight back onto her phone and checked to see if she had got accepted by anyone on Facebook or if she had been accepted into any of the groups she wanted to join.

When she logged back onto Facebook, she noticed that she had loads of friend requests from people she didn't know and there were some really fit guys who also added her, so she checked out their profiles to see if she knew anyone on their profile or to see if it was a scam and there were people who just added her to make fun of her.

Luckily, the people who added Patrice was no one from school and she got accepted to all the groups she asked to join and one of them groups was called "I hate being a loner and I just want to make friends"

While Patrice was searching for some more people to add, she found she had a friend request from this bloke who she had never heard off before so she decided to search through his profile to see who he was and what he did for a living and then she found out it was someone she knew when she was at Sunday school with, but she couldn't remember him as he was friends with Terry.

Patrice decided to send him a message, "Hi Darren how's you? I can't believe you sent me a friends request as you never spoke to me during Sunday school."

Once she sent the message it was just a waiting game now just to see if he would respond to her message.

It was getting near teatime and her parents would be home soon, so she decided to cook them all Tuna Pasta Bake and it would hopefully be ready for when her parents got back.

After an hour of Patrice preparing dinner and washing the pots, her parents came back, "Hi darling how did you do today on your mock exams with Mr Connel?"

Patrice looked at her parents with a smile on her face, "I think I passed my English exam, but Mr Connel had to get back to school before we could mark the Maths exam, so I don't know how I did on that one."

Charlotte and Andrew looked at each other with a smile on their faces, "Oh darling well done we knew you could do it as your spelling is good and you're always correcting me when I have written a sentence when it sounds wrong. I got to say well done as well for preparing and cooking tea as it smells yummy, so thank you."

Patrice smiled back at her parents, "Well let's get tucked in before it gets cold, and I hope you both like it."

After they all had tea, everyone couldn't stop yawning so they all went up to bed and Patrice read a book she was interested in, and she also checked Facebook again before she went to sleep to see if Darren had replied but there was still no answer.

CHAPTER 24

The next morning, Patrice heard her phone buzzing, so she quickly got her phone and checked who it was, and it was Darren who messaged her back, "Morning hope I didn't wake you, and sorry for the late reply, I work nights you see as a security guard on a building site. I was mega busy last night, and I didn't even have time to check my phone. But yes, I do remember you as you kept on looking at me and Terry during one of the services at church, but I couldn't do anything about it back then as I was seeing someone, but I am now young, free, and single so thought I would message you to see if you wanted to meet up if you're not seeing anyone. I am off to bed now but feel free to reply and I will check it when I wake up."

Patrice didn't know what to do as she fancied Terry but now after that message from Darren, she didn't know how to feel, so she sent a message back to Darren, "Thanks for the reply back as I was getting a bit worried that you wouldn't reply, I am sort of seeing Terry now but I have not heard from him in a while so I don't know what's happening there, but I will find out and yes I would love to meet up with you again and have a catch up. Hope you sleep well."

Patrice decided to get up and go for a shower, but when she opened her bedroom door, she noticed that the bathroom was occupied and she could hear these weird noises coming from the bathroom, so she went to her parent's room to have a look to see if they were awake but no one was in there, so she figured that she would go downstairs and check on Shaky and go back up for a shower later.

When she got downstairs, and checked up on Shaky, she noticed that she didn't have any of her food that she gave her last night, so she ran to the bottom of the stairs, "MUM, DAD COME QUICK I think there is something wrong with Shaky as she didn't eat any of her food I put out for her last night, and I am worried."

Charlotte poked her head out of the bathroom door, "Okay, darling try not to panic as its normal for dogs to be off their food but let me just get my dressing gown back on and I will come down and have a look at her."

Patrice rushed back to get too Shaky, so she wasn't by herself, and when she got back to her, she noticed that she wasn't breathing normal, and she started to cry her eyes out.

Within five minutes of Patrice shouting her parents, they both came down and ran straight to the conservatory where Shaky sleeps, "Andrew get the phone quick and ring the vets up as Patrice is right, she is not breathing properly, and I will go and get my mobile and ring in work and tell them I can't go in today as we have a family emergency."

Charlotte ran back up to her bedroom and goes and gets her phone, but no one was in the office so she left a message on the answer phone "Hi it's Charlotte Umar ringing, I hate to do this to you at the last minute, but we have had a family emergency and I can't come into work today I am afraid."

Charlotte rushed back downstairs to be with her daughter who was incredibly stressed and went to sit next to her and gave her a hug, "Don't worry darling we will get Shaky sorted and me and your dad love her very much as she's family."

As soon as Charlotte stood up, she felt a pain in her stomach and then she noticed that her waters had broken, "Andrew, have you got off that phone to the vets yet, as I need another favour but if you still on the phone, I will ring my parents."

Andrew came rushing back to where they were all sitting with Shaky, and nearly slipped over as the floor was wet "I am off the phone now, don't tell me Shaky did a wee on the floor as I nearly just slipped over rushing back to you both."

Patrice pointed to where her mum was sitting, "Look dad, mum's waters have broken, and we need to get an ambulance. I will ring granddad and ask him to come down and sit with me in case we have to take Shaky to the vets and you go to the hospital with mum."

Andrew didn't know what to do as he was in a right panic as he was worried about Shaky and he was also worried about his wife, "Right I better phone for an ambulance and Patrice ring granddad for me please and explain the situation for me please."

Charlotte yelled while looking at her family, "There is no time for an ambulance as the baby is coming now, Patrice can you go and get me some water and some towels please. Andrew, can you try and take me into the living room, so I can sit on the carpet as I don't want to have the baby in the cold conservatory."

Patrice rushed to get the towels for her mum and some water while Andrew tried his best to take his wife into the living room where it was a bit warmer. But while Patrice was rushing around, she put her granddad on loudspeaker, "Hi grandad how's you and grandma? Hope you're free as we could really do with your help as mum's gone into labour and Shaky is not very well as she is not breathing, and there is no time for dad to ring for an ambulance either as the baby is coming."

Paul sounded shocked and excited, "Right, darling, don't worry, me and your grandma will come straight away as your grandma wouldn't want to miss the birth of her grandchild even though she was going to go to bingo, but she just told me that she will come with me and that she can go to bingo any time."

As soon as Patrice thanked her grandparent for coming over, she rushed into the living room to see how her mum was, "How you doing mum, and dad what did the vet say about Shaky?"

Andrew had a puzzled look on his face as he thought he told them about the vets, "Don't worry darling they are going to send a vet round to check her over, darling can you do mummy a favour please, as I have to stay at the bottom end in case the baby comes, can you keep tapping your mum's forehead with a wet towel please as that would be a great help."

Patrice did as she was asked as she didn't want her mum to be in a pain, after a minute of Patrice dabbing her mum's forehead, her grandparents walked through the door, "Hi darling we are here now, I saw the vet outside, so I let her in I will take her straight to Shaky for you and we will give you all some privacy."

Paul and Gabbie took the vet into the conservatory where Shaky was lying down and for the vet to check her over.

The vet got her equipment out and started to give Shaky a once over, "I am glad to say that there is nothing wrong with her but the only reason why she is off her food is because she can feel the tension in everyone and how things are going as she could tell there was a problem with everyone, meaning all the stress and things like that just got to her, animals feel things just as much as us humans."

Paul shouted to his family, "Good news Shaky is fine she could just sense the tension in the house and everything."

After he shouted that, he heard Andrew say to Charlotte, "Right darling you just need to do one more push than it's all over."

Charlotte gave the biggest push that she could and then within a few minutes she gave birth to a little boy. Patrice went running into where her grandparents were, "I have a baby brother, I think I will give my parents some alone time for a bit and come and check on Shaky to see if she's perked up a bit."

Paul and Gabbie looked at Patrice, "Has anyone rang for the ambulance as your mum will have to go and get checked over at the hospital."

Patrice looked at her grandparents again and had a long thought, "To be honest, think my dad was about to ring 999 but then my mum said it was too late and that my brother was coming."

Anne looked at Patrice with a smile on her face, "Congratulations on being a big sister, and where is Shakey's food, please as we can try and feed her again and see if she eats?"

Patrice went and fetched her food and took it to Anne, "Here is her food do you want me to put some food in her bowl for you? Before I go back to see my little brother?"

Anne shook her head and Patrice went back into the living room, "Dad did you manage to ring for an ambulance for mum, as granddad and grandma said its best that she goes into hospital to get checked over?"

Andrew looked at his wife, "It's up to you darling did you want me to ring the midwife up and explain that you have given birth and to see if you need to go into hospital?"

Charlotte looked down at her baby then back to her family, "I know, all I want to do now is sleep, but then again we don't have the cot set up or anything and it's also up to you Andrew what do you think?"

Andrew didn't know what to do for the best, so he got onto the midwife, "Hello is this the midwife for Mrs Umar? I thought I better ring you to just check something with you. My wife has given birth to a beautiful little boy at home, and we wondered if she would have to go to hospital, but she did say she was so drained and all that she wanted to do was sleep."

The midwife, Betsy replied, "Well that's completely up to both of you, but I will have to come round and do a check to see if the baby is okay and also if mother is doing well. I have to make sure all of the afterbirth is out. I will be round as soon as possible; I am only round the corner from you."

Andrew looked at his wife, "Yes please if that's okay as we would love to know how much he weighs and that, please, as at the moment my wife has just fallen asleep on the floor, and we have managed to clean everywhere up as well, and my daughter has cleaned up her brother as well."

Betsy looked at her notes while she was on the phone, "Okay, Mr Umar I am on my way, and I will be two to three minutes approx."

After five minutes of Betsy saying that, she arrived at the house, Andrew went to let her in, "Thank you for coming so quick, as we didn't expect her to give birth today as we thought we had another few days until she was going to be induced."

Betsy got the things out that she needed and then she went into the living room where Charlotte was lying with the baby. "Congratulations to both of you on the birth of your little boy, have you got a name yet for him as he's absolutely gorgeous?"

Andrew looked at Charlotte and said, "Paddy after Charlotte's great granddad."

Charlotte couldn't believe that Andrew chose that name as she thought he hated it, "Darling, I thought you hated that name? I thought we were going to go with your middle name, Rick?"

While Charlotte and Andrew were discussing names, Betsy picked up the little boy and put him on the scales to see how much he weighed, "I am pleased to say that he weighs 5lb 8oz and he's looking good as well."

Charlotte looked at Betsy, "Would it be possible to stay at home as I don't like hospitals that much as I had a bad experience when I had Patrice."

Betsy nodded and went over to where Patrice was, "I see you did a grand job with cleaning your little brother up when your mum gave birth."

Patrice smiled and went over to where her parents were and left her grandparents with Shaky, "I will do anything in my power to make sure my little bro has the best start in life as I am so pleased with my parents as they did a fantastic job with everything as my dad was a star."

Paul and Gabbie came in to have a look at the new baby and they were so smitten, "Right darling me and your mum better leave you all alone for a bit and congratulations to all of you and don't worry about Shaky we can take her with us for a few days if that will make your life easier as you will have your hands full with this little one,"

Charlotte got up and gave her parents a massive hug, "Thank you, both of you for being here and looking after Shaky for us for a few days we will sort out some food and toys for her as well."

Patrice got right onto that even though she was a bit sad that Shaky wouldn't be at home much but then again, she knew it was best since she now has a baby brother at home. "I will just go and fetch everything you need granddad."

Once Patrice fetched everything that Paul and Gabbie needed, she gave Shaky a big kiss and a cuddle, "Don't worry we will see you in a few days and I will come and visit you every day."

After Paul and Gabbie left and once Betsy checked over the baby to make sure he was okay she looked at both Charlotte and Andrew, "Don't worry Charlotte you don't need to go into hospital if you don't want to as I have known a few mums who feel the same as you. I am more than happy to let you stay at home with your family."

While everything was going mad in the house with a newborn baby, Patrice went to check on Winston the parrot as with all the excitement she forgot to go and check on him, "Morning Winston how are you? Sorry I haven't been to see you for a few days, but I know dad has been looking after you as I have been busy looking after Shaky."

Winston looked at Patrice and went to sit on her arm, "Morning" and gave her a peck on the cheek as that's the way he gives everyone kisses.

Once Patrice checked up on Winston, she shut the conservatory door and let him fly around for a while as he hasn't been out of his cage for a few days which is not good as she knew that parrots had to be out of their cages a couple of days so they could spread their wings.

Once Patrice left Winston, she went to see her parents, "Mum can I hold my little brother please, I would say his name, but I heard you and dad discussing names, but I didn't know which one you went for."

Charlotte looked at her daughter with a sort of smirk on her face, "Darling I think we are going to go with Paddy after my great granddad who was a big part of my life as he used to look after me when it was the holidays when I was in school and of course you can hold your little brother."

Patrice sat down next to her mum and Charlotte put some cushions under Patrice's arms then placed Paddy on Patrice for a short while because Paddy was getting hungry.

While Patrice was holding Paddy, Charlotte quickly got her phone and took a picture of her kids as she was so happy now that her family was complete. "Mum, can I have a copy of that picture please so I can put it on my Facebook if that's okay?"

Charlotte smiled at her daughter, "Of course darling I was going to do that myself as well."

While Patrice was holding her brother, Charlotte got ready to feed Paddy, "Darling I am afraid it's time for his feed now, and I will have to take him, but you can have another hold of him later if we don't get a house full later."

Patrice looked puzzled, "Why do you think we will get a house full later? Do you think some of the family will come round today as I know granddad Paul and grandma Gabbie knows about Paddy, but I don't know about my other grandparents knowing unless dad has told them?"

Charlotte looked at her daughter with a smile on her face, "I think dad was going to tell his parents, but I am not sure has; he had to rush to work as they called him in for a meeting, I am just praying that he can get maternity leave as well."

Patrice smiled back to her mum while she was feeding Paddy, "Mum I have just had a thought? Does your workplace know that you have given birth?"

Charlotte had a long think about what Patrice just asked her, "You have just reminded me I have to let work know, darling can I ask you a huge favour please while I am feeding your brother can you ring my work place up for me, please and ask for Peter."

Patrice nodded and went to get the house phone to ring her mum's workplace, "Hello it's Mrs Umar's daughter Patrice ringing up on her behalf as she cannot come to the phone at the moment."

Yolanda answered the phone as she was on the front desk replied, "Oh hi Patrice how are you feeling as I have heard you haven't been feeling yourself recently? How can I help you?"

Patrice replied with a big smile on her face as she was so excited in what had happened today, "My mum has asked me to let you all know that she has given birth to a beautiful little boy called Paddy after her great granddad and that she wanted to know about maternity leave please?"

Yolanda sounded shocked as she didn't think Charlotte was going on leave till next week, "Oh congratulation all of you, I will put you through to the manager Peter and he can let you know the facts."

Yolanda put Patrice through to Peter, "Hello Patrice, how are you today? Hope your family are fine? I hear congratulations are in order as Yolanda just told me. The answer to your question is roughly six months but she might be able to get a bit longer off depends how Paddy is, but it will be at a reduced rate of pay though. But I can certainly have a look into it for her. Give her all our best please."

Patrice smiled to herself, "Thanks Peter I will let my mum know and of course I will give her all your best."

Once Patrice got off the phone to her mum's boss, she went back into the living room where Charlotte was breastfeeding Paddy, "Mum I have just spoken to Peter and he sends everyone from your workplace their best and he also said it's normally six months, but you might be able to get a bit longer off depends how Paddy is, but it will be at a reduced rate of pay though. But he said he can certainly have a look into it for you."

After Charlotte finished breastfeeding Paddy, she put him back into his Moses basket as he fell asleep during his feed, "Thanks for that darling, I appreciate it and glad Peter is going to look into it for me."

Patrice smiled back at her mum then she put some pictures of her brother on her social media while her mum was getting some shut eye on the sofa.

After Patrice posted some pictures of her brother on Facebook, she decided to then go back to check on Winston to see if he's okay, but when she arrived in the conservatory, she found him back in his cage drinking some water, so she decided to fill up his feed. Winston made a light happy noise as if to say thank you for feeding him. Patrice scratched his feathery neck and shut the cage.

Once she shut Winston back in his cage, she came back to where her parents were, "How are you feeling now mum, as you got me so worried earlier? But glad dad is here now."

Charlotte looked at her husband as she wanted to know if he had told work about Paddy, "Darling I forgot to ask you, did you tell work that we now have a son and to see if you could take some leave?"

Andrew completely forgot to let his manager know about Paddy with the phone call from his daughter about her mum and the meeting, "No sorry hunny bun I forgot but I will ring my manager now and explain everything."

Andrew got his mobile out of his coat pocket, "Hello Mr Ping it's Andrew Umar here, sorry I had to leave so quickly it was because my wife was unwell, and Patrice had to ring for an ambulance. The reason why I am ringing is because I forgot to let everyone know yesterday at the meeting that my lovely wife gave birth to our lovely little boy called Paddy and I was wondering if I get any sort of leave to help her out, please sir?"

Mr Ping sounded shocked, "Oh Andrew I am so sorry to hear about your wife, hope she is well today. To be honest I was going to ring you this morning as I saw the pictures on Facebook that Charlotte put up and tagged you in and I must say he looks so cute. Congratulations and from what I can remember you get two weeks leave hope that is sufficient?"

Andrew didn't even notice that his wife put any pictures on Facebook or even tagged him in any. "Oh, thank you so much Sir I appreciate it and my mobile is always on if you need me for anything as I can work from home as well if you need me to."

After Andrew got off the phone he went straight to his wife in the living room, "Guess what darling, I get 2 weeks off and I didn't even know you put photos up of Paddy and tagged me in them as Mr Ping told me about it and he sends his congratulations as well to us all."

Charlotte looked shocked as she was certain that she sent her husband a text, "Let me just check my mobile as I am 100% certain I text you to let you know, as I also said that Patrice could post some pictures as well."

Once Charlotte checked her phone to see if she pressed send, she noticed that she forgot, "Oh Darling I did start to type the text, but I must have forgotten to press send, I am so sorry."

It was getting near to teatime, and everyone had been so busy that day that they all forgot to have lunch, and everyone was so tired as they had all been busy doing their own things at home, Andrew had a thought, "Why don't I order us all a Chinese for tea just us lot for tonight then we can all have a good night's sleep after."

Charlotte and Patrice looked at each other then they both shouted, "WHAT A GREAT IDEA AS I AM SO HUNGRY THAT I CAN EAT A HORSE CAN WE HAVE THE NORMAL PLEASE?"

After Andrew placed the order, he went to fetch it as he refused to pay for delivery as that would have been £1.50 extra and now that Paddy is here, they needed to tighten their belts a bit more.

While Charlotte and Patrice were waiting for Andrew to come back with the food, Charlotte fed Paddy again and she took him upstairs into his cot. She then set the table while Patrice checked her Facebook to see if she had any messages from Darren.

When she logged onto Facebook, she noticed that Darren had poked her and sent her a message, "**Hi Patrice hope you're doing well, congratulations on your new arrival by the way and I was wondering if you fancied going out some time, I know you're seeing Terry but to be honest I have something bad to tell you about him as well but that is for another day. I will wait for your reply.**"

Patrice couldn't believe what she had just read, so she sent a reply saying, "**Sure I would love to meet up with you and please tell me what you need to tell me about Terry as I am worried as I have not heard anything from him for a while, I am free most of this week but then next week I am back at school and thanks.**"

Once Patrice replied to Darren her dad turned up with the food, everyone was so hungry that it didn't take them long to eat their tea.

Patrice cleared everything away and put on the dishwasher then they all went to bed, "Night mum and dad, sleep well and give my little bro a big kiss from his sister please."

Charlotte nodded then they shut their bedroom door and Patrice went to her bedroom as well and checked her messages before she went to sleep, and noticed that Darren had replied, "**I don't know if I should tell you really, but I saw Terry with another girl, and they seemed madly in love with each other. And I am glad you said you would go out with me one day, why don't we meet up tomorrow as I have a day off work?**"

Patrice had a long hard thought on what to reply as she was mad at Terry for apparently seeing someone behind her back, of course in her heart she was livid; but on the other hand, she was pleased as she fancied Darren more anyway. "**Oh, Darren I would love to go out somewhere with you tomorrow and by the way who is this Terry you keep mentioning as I don't know anyone called Terry anymore as he's dead to me as I have not heard anything from him in ages and guess I won't hear anything from him now if he's got another girl.**"

CHAPTER 25

The next morning, Patrice woke up with a huge smile on her face before she got out of bed, she decided to check her phone to see if she had heard anything else from Darren.

She was so pleased that Darren had messaged her back, "**Morning sweet cheeks hope you slept well, I slept like a log last night after our conversation and you agreeing to go out with me later today and I cannot wait to go out with you as I have something special planned.**"

Patrice jumped out of bed and quickly went into the shower before her parents got there first. Once she had her shower she went downstairs and made everyone breakfast as she was so happy things were going right in her life at the moment, so she thought.

While she was preparing breakfast for everyone, her phone rang, "Hello Terry, nice of you to ring me since you ain't even spoken to me for God knows how long. What do I owe this pleasure?"

Terry sounded shocked as he thought Patrice would be pleased to hear from him, "What's up Pat, why are you not pleased to hear from me? I will just get straight to the point, you know I really loved you, don't you? The thing is, the age gap was part of the problem and that you were a virgin when I first met you, which is good. But I have heard loads of things about you which I wasn't keen on; you told me that you never been with anyone before, then I heard different" Patrice heard Terry sigh sadly down the end of the phone. "Well, I will just get straight to it, I am seeing someone else, and I can't see you anymore, I am so sorry Patrice!"

Patrice started to cry down the phone, "Why are you listening to other people for and why didn't you just come straight to me and ask me before listening to gossip. Anyway, it doesn't matter as I am going on a date later today anyway but thanks for ringing me up have a nice life, Terry." Patrice spat, but adding the information about the date, she felt that she had won.

Once she put the phone on Terry, she carried on making breakfast for everyone and after a few minutes of her preparing breakfast it was ready, "Mum, Dad, breakfast is ready come and get it."

Andrew came downstairs first, "Oh darling you didn't have to make us breakfast, it looks yummy though, but we will have to put your mums in the oven as she is feeding Paddy at the minute, but she won't be long. What's up darling it looks like you have been crying?"

Patrice sat next to her dad while they were eating breakfast, "It's fine, dad, don't worry, but all I will say is that I am going on a date later with Darren. He used to go to our church as he added me on Facebook when I joined up and we have been messaging each other ever since. Hope that's okay with you, dad?"

Andrew looked at his daughter with a smile on his face, "Don't be silly darling of course it's okay for you to go out on a date. If I am honest, I didn't really like Terry." Andrew pulled out his wallet and rifled through. "Hmm... anyway here is thirty for you to take with you and go and enjoy yourself."

Patrice gave her dad a big hug then she went up to see her mum, "Morning mum how are you today? How's Paddy? I have made you some breakfast which is in the oven for you so it can stay warm. Can I have a hold of Paddy please mum, if he is awake as I don't want to wake him."

Charlotte looked at Patrice, "What's the matter darling your eyes are red, have you been crying? And he is asleep now but when he wakes up for his next feed later you can have a hold of him then."

Patrice nodded in agreement and went to go and get ready for her going out with Darren later. "Mum" she shouted, "can I borrow you for a moment please before you go down and have your breakfast. I'm in my bedroom and need your advice on something!"

Charlotte got out of bed as quietly as she could, so she didn't wake Paddy up, then she shut the door so quietly and went to Patrice's bedroom to see what she needed help with, "Don't yell, remember baby in the house now." "Sorry mum. "It's okay but what's up darling, what can I help you with?"

Patrice showed her mum some lovely clothes that she picked out to go out in with Darren later that day, "Mum I am going on a date later with Darren who I knew when we were at church and he's taking me out, but I can't decide on what to wear?"

Charlotte looked shocked as she thought her daughter was going out with Terry, "Oh I thought you were going out with Terry as you both seemed so smitten with each other when you were both here what's happened and is that why you were crying?"

Patrice turned to face her mum, "Oh mum, I can't believe how stupid I was thinking Terry fancied me and wanted to go out with me, he is seeing someone else now and he don't want to see me again as he heard some rumours about me, and he didn't like them."

Charlotte started to cry as she thought all the rumours had stopped about her daughter, "Oh darling I am so sorry to hear that, but I am glad you're getting on with your life and not letting this sort of thing bother you here is twenty for you to take out with you and for you to enjoy yourself with."

Patrice hugged her mum and kissed her on the cheek, "Thanks mum, I now have £50 as dad gave me £30 as well and Darren is a lot better than Terry anyway but the only thing is I don't know where he's taking me so I can't decide on what to wear."

Charlotte looked at Patrice with a weird look, "Oh darling you will look wonderful in whatever you decide to wear, and Darren is one lucky fella to be taking a wonderful, kind and beautiful young girl out like yourself."

Patrice gave her mum a big kiss and decided to go with a nice blouse and some jeggers for her date.

After an hour of Patrice getting ready, her phone rang, "Hi Darren is everything okay? I am nearly ready where am I meeting you?"

Darren didn't expect Patrice to say that as he never even said a time to her, "Hi Patrice I was just ringing to see where you wanted to go? I did have an idea but where I wanted to take us, they are fully booked up."

Patrice looked at the time on her watch, "What time are you picking me up by the way as I am ready and waiting for you, but Paddy has just woken up for his next feed and my mum said I can hold him before she feeds him, why don't you come and wait for me at mine, and you can sit in the living room?"

Darren sounded shocked as he was already outside her house and he didn't know how to let her know, "Okay thanks...um, I am actually outside yours now and I will come and head to the front door now."

Patrice screamed into her sleeve and went running to her parents who were downstairs now, "Please you two don't ask too many questions to Darren as he's just about to come to the door and I still need to get my makeup on and do my hair can someone let him in please?"

Patrice rushed back to her bedroom and put some makeup on and even styled her hair which she never does, and her dad went to let Darren in, "Hi

Darren I am Andrew Umar, it's a pleasure to meet you and this is my wife, Charlotte; please come in and take a seat I think Patrice is finishing off getting ready."

Darren nodded and took his shoes and coat off and went to sit in the living room with her dad, "This is a nice place you have here Sir, and oh by the way congratulations of the birth of you son I have heard a lot about him from Patrice as she never shuts up about him which is really nice."

Charlotte headed upstairs to see Paddy and to see how Patrice was getting on, "Darling, Darren is here, and he is sat with your dad in the living room, and I am just about to feed Paddy if you want a quick hold before you go out as I know he would love to see his big sister."

Patrice quickly finished putting her makeup on and went into her parent's room where Paddy was lying in his cot and picked him up, "Oh my dear Paddy you're so beautiful and you will break everyone's heart when you get older, I love you so much and never forget that."

Just before she hands him over to her mum, she gave Paddy a kiss on the cheeky and started to blow raspberries to him which made him laugh.

Charlotte came and stood near to where Patrice was standing with Paddy, "You better go now darling as you can't be too careful in what your dad might ask Darren."

Patrice ran down the stairs and, on a few occasions, she nearly tripped but she managed to grab the handrail quickly before she did fall. "Hi Darren, sorry I took ages I am ready now for your date or whatever this is."

Darren couldn't believe how sexy Patrice looked, "Oh Patrice you're stunning I am one lucky fella taking you out. We can either go and catch a film or we can go for something to eat somewhere nice in the city as I have my dad's sports car."

Patrice was shocked as she loved sports cars a lot, "Oh wow Darren your dad has a sports car what sort is it has it got a soft top as I love them sort of cars. I don't mind what we do I don't even mind just going for a drive somewhere and see where it takes us."

While Charlotte was breastfeeding Paddy, she felt bad that she couldn't go downstairs to meet Darren, "Have a great time you two and be safe; and Patrice don't be back to late and if you are please try and be quiet when you come in, in case we are asleep."

Patrice agreed and they both went to Darren's car and Patrice couldn't actually believe that it was a soft top after all and she was so excited, "Do you want the hood down Patrice and let the wind blow in your hair?"

Patrice nodded and Darren put the soft top down and they just drove away into the sunset but they still didn't know where to go until Darren saw a lovely nature reserve which he parked in for a little bit so they could just sit and chat about things.

Patrice was not very comfortable in doing this, "Sorry to be a spoil sport Darren but can we go someplace else please as I have had bad experience here before and I don't want them coming back to haunt me if that's okay?"

Darren looked shocked at Patrice, "I know, don't worry I am not taking you here, as your dad told me about what had happened to you when you were a young girl, we are actually going in the building next door which is a lovely hotel and I have booked us a room for the night and don't worry your dad knows as well as I had to ask his permission before I brought you here as I didn't want to get into any trouble for doing this and there is a lovely restaurant in here as well we can go to."

Patrice was gobsmacked as she has never been allowed to stay in a hotel before with a fella and she was also shocked that her dad agreed to this as well. "Are you sure my dad actually agreed for me to stay here with you tonight as my mum is set against this sort of thing and I also thought my dad was as well."

Darren looked at Patrice before he got out of the car and opened Patrice's door, "Yes, your dad agreed to this as I think he wants to have some quality time with your mum and Paddy as he knows he has to go back to work in just over a week and don't worry its two single beds in the room."

Patrice was over the moon about this as she had always wanted to stay in a hotel with someone before, "I can't wait now, and I am so hungry it's unreal." They both chuckled as Darren's stomach joined in to say he was hungry to.

Darren went to open Patrice's side door to let her out and then they went up to the entrance of the hotel and Darren went up to the front desk, "Afternoon my name is Mr Darren Brewood, and I rang up this morning to book a room for the night with single beds in there please."

The receptionist checked on her computer, "Oh yes Mr Brewood I have found your booking but unfortunately, we couldn't get one with two single beds in I am afraid, but it has got a bed settee in there and a single bed if that's any good for you?"

Darren looked over at Patrice, who was on the phone to her parents, "Hi mum, dad, you will never believe where Darren has brought me?"

Andrew didn't know what to say in front of Charlotte, so he held up a finger, took the phone off speaker, and went into another room, "I know darling, promise me one thing and be safe. If he pushes you into anything you don't want to do and he doesn't listen, you shout until your lungs burst and ring me straight away; I will come and pick you up. Your mum still doesn't know where he's taken you just yet as I have not had time to tell her, but do you want me to pass the phone to her so you can tell her?

Patrice didn't dare really tell her mum, but she agreed with her dad, "Okay then dad I will tell her if your chicken to tell mum the truth." She laughed as Andrew came back into the living room.

Andrew passed the phone to Charlotte, "Hi mum how's Paddy? You will never believe where Darren has brought me? It's a lovely hotel in the countryside and he's paid for a room for us tonight but don't worry its single beds but in one room and he's taking us out for a nice romantic meal later and he also asked dads permission beforehand as well and he agreed to let him bring me here."

Charlotte gave Andrew a horrible stare, "Paddy is okay, thanks darling. Oh, did he now darling, but I wish your dad asked me as well before he agreed to this, but what is done is done now just be careful won't you and if Darren tries anything and you don't like it just ring me or your father UNDERSTOOD?"

Patrice agreed, "I know mum, dad has already given me the talk and told me the same thing. Give Paddy a big kiss from me and I will see you both tomorrow, love you both."

After Patrice got off the phone, they both went up to the room and Patrice realised that she didn't have any spare clothes, "I don't have any nice clothes to wear as I have only got what I have come in and I look a right tramp."

Darren looked at Patrice with a sort of smirk on his face, "Don't worry about that, I have brought you some new clothes for this special occasion. To be honest I didn't know where to take you 'till, I was outside your door in the car as my mum suggested this place in fact to me while I was on the phone to her waiting for your reply."

Patrice looked shocked as no one has ever done this sort of thing for her before, "Oh Darren they are lovely how much I owe you for the clothes as I have some cash; please let me pay you for them?"

Darren shook his head, "No need to pay me for them as I wanted to treat you and my mum actually picked the clothes out as I am no good at picking out women's clothes."

They both got changed and got ready to go down for something to eat in the restaurant called "The Mergim."

Patrice couldn't believe how lovely it was in the restaurant and she was so gobsmacked that she couldn't stop looking at the decorations, "Oh Darren this restaurant is so lovely, and it looks expensive let's split the bill this time as it's not fair you paying for the food as well as the room."

Darren agreed this time for Patrice to go halves with him and after they had a lovely meal they went back up to the room and watched some television only because Patrice was not old enough to drink in a bar yet and Darren had brought some alcohol with him for the pair of them to drink in the room.

CHAPTER 26

The next morning, Patrice woke up first so she decided to make them both a cup of tea and she also ordered some room service to bring them some breakfast up so they could have something to eat in the bedroom even though the restaurant was open she didn't feel up to going downstairs, "Morning Darren did you sleep well I have made us both a cup of tea but I didn't know if you had sugar so I left the sugar out of your cup for you."

Darren opened one eye as he was still half asleep, "Morning Patrice how did you sleep last night? I slept like a log. I don't have sugar in my tea as I am sweet enough; think we better get ready to go and get some breakfast before we head back."

While Darren was talking there was a knock on the door, "Room service I have brought your breakfast up for you, I will leave it outside the door for you."

Patrice went to get the breakfast, "I beat you to it as I placed an order just now for them to bring it up to us as I had a lovely evening; so, this morning I thought we could have our last meal in here before I have to go back home."

Darren couldn't believe that Patrice did something like this, "Oh Patrice you're a gem it's a lovely idea. I know we don't really know each other that well although we did go to the same church when we were younger, but I have something I want to ask you."

Patrice took a mouthful of her bacon, "Okay then ask away I am all ears."

Darren stopped what he was doing and faced her, "I know we have been talking for a few days now but not actually met up properly till last night, but I think I know everything I need to know about you, and I know this might sound a bit sudden, but will you do me the honour of marrying me?"

Patrice stopped what she was doing, and she looked a bit puzzled, "Are you having a laugh as we don't really know each other that well; it's only been a few days that we have been talking. I don't mean to sound nasty or owt as I would love nothing more than to marry you but it's a bit too soon. If I agreed, we would have to keep it a secret for a little while."

Darren was shocked, "So does that mean you won't marry me then?"

Patrice went over to where Darren was sitting, "I didn't say yes and I didn't say no. I just said if I agreed to marry you, we will have to keep it a secret for a little while; can I just think about it for a bit, please?"

Darren agreed and Patrice went to get a shower and to freshen up before they headed back home. While Patrice was in the shower, she started to sing a random song that she just made up and Darren never heard her sing before, so he went to have a listen at the bathroom door.

Once Patrice finished in the shower, Darren rushed back to where he was sitting, so she didn't know he was listening to her singing. "Have you got an answer for me yet, not that I am pushing you for an answer?"

Patrice looked at Darren and went to sit opposite from him as she needed to dry her hair, "Okay, I have thought about it and the answer is YES I will marry you, but can we keep it between ourselves for the time being please, as I don't even have a ring yet."

Darren was shocked that Patrice had agreed to marry him, so he went up to where she was and gave her a big hug, "Am I dreaming or something as I can't believe that you actually said yes. I am gobsmacked as I thought you would have said no;

you don't know how much you have made me happy right now."

Patrice looked at Darren, "I know I have shocked myself as well, and to be honest I am glad I said yes as you're so thoughtful and so exceedingly kind and I knew this from day one. As all the other blokes I have met are all twats and never treated me with the respect like you have. So, thank you for making me the happiest women right now."

After they both got ready, they decided to go for a nice walk around the nature reserve, but before they left Patrice said, "I need to ring my parents and let them know that I will be back a bit later if that's okay, if we are going for a walk?"

Darren nodded his head, "Okay then, while you ring your parents, I will take our stuff down to the car and meet you outside."

Patrice nodded to Darren and got straight onto her phone, "Hi mum, just to let you know that I had a lovely evening and we have decided to go for a walk round the nature reserve if that's okay with you and dad?"

Charlotte sounded half asleep, "Morning darling, glad you had a lovely evening and that's fine with us, but don't be too late please as we are thinking of taking Paddy out today but only when you get back."

Patrice smiled down the phone to her mum, "Don't worry I won't be too long as we just needed to go for a nice walk as we ate to much last night and we both feel fat" she chuckled, "I will only be an hour or so."

Once Patrice got off the phone to her mum, she went to meet Darren outside the hotel, and they went for a nice stroll around the river and sat down halfway round for a little rest.

After they sat down for a little while, Patrice noticed that she had a text on her phone from her parents, "Hi Darling, we are thinking of going out in the next half hour if you wanted to come with us can you come now, please, as we are just waiting for you to come back now."

Once Patrice saw the text message, she looked at Darren, "I don't mean to sound rude or anything, but my parents are wanting to take my baby brother out for a stroll, and she wanted to know if I wanted to go which I do. Sorry, would you mind if we headed back to mine now, please, as I want to go out with them if you don't mind."

Darren looked at his watch as he wanted to know what time it was as he was getting hungry anyway, "Of course I can drop you back off home now, to be honest I am getting a bit hungry myself and my parents want to see me for a bit anyway."

They both headed back to Darren's car, once they got back to the car, Darren leaned towards Patrice and gave her a big kiss on the lips which she didn't expect, "Oh Darren I didn't expect that, and you gave me a fright." She smiled and chuckled quietly.

Darren looked shocked as he thought she knew he wanted to give her a kiss, he opened Patrice' side of the car and let her in as he was a proper gentleman.

Once they arrived at Patrice's house, Patrice leaned over and gave him a kiss, "Thanks for a wonderful night and I have enjoyed myself a lot hope we can meet up again soon."

Darren turned to Patrice after she gave him a quick goodbye kiss, "You're more than welcome as I enjoyed myself as well, you have made me the happiest lad alive right now."

Patrice hurried back inside the house so she could get ready to take Paddy out with her parents, "Mum, Dad I won't be long I am just going to get changed then I will be downstairs then we can all go out as a family."

Charlotte carried on getting Paddy ready and making sure that she had got everything like nappies, bottles, and a warm blanket as it was cold outside. "Hurry up please darling as me and your dad are ready to go, we will wait outside for you but don't be long."

Patrice hurried up in getting changed, but while she was trying to get her bottoms on, she fell over and hurt herself, "OUCH that really hurt" she yelped thinking one of her parents would hear her, but they didn't, so she got up of the floor and carried on getting ready.

After a few more moments of getting ready she eventually came downstairs, "I am ready, but I had a bit of a blonde moment; while I was getting my bottoms on, I fell over and I am surprised neither of you heard me shouting."

Charlotte looked at Andrew then they both looked at their daughter, "No we are sorry sweetheart we didn't hear a thing but are you okay though?"

Patrice laughed at her parents, "Of course I am okay, it was just a little fall and I landed on some cushions on the floor but banged my head a little bit. Don't worry I am fine though."

While they were all out having a family stroll, they decided to go to the park to feed the ducks when it started to snow, "Oh wow look, it's snowing! I love the snow but shame it is not deep enough to make a snowman yet."

Charlotte didn't know what to say apart from, "I think we better get Paddy back home as it's getting cold, and I haven't brought anything thick enough to cover him over with as I didn't expect it to snow while we were out."

They all agreed, and they headed back home, but while they were walking home, they bumped into Andrew's mum and stepdad, "Hello, you two, how you both doing, not heard from you in a while. We are just heading back home as it started to snow, and we haven't got anything to cover Paddy up with. Say, why don't you both come back with us, and we can all have a catch up and you can meet your grandson."

Samantha looked at George who then looked at Paddy, "That would be lovely thanks, son. I could do with a little cuddle from my grandson as he's so cute. Has Paul and Gabbie meet him yet?"

Andrew looked at his wife with a worried look on his face, "Actually mum, yes, they did meet Paddy but that is only because on the day he was born they were coming to pick up Shaky as she was not feeling to good and the vet came round to check on her and Charlotte's waters broke and it gave us all a shock as she was meant to be going in *this* week to get induced and it all happened so fast, she gave birth at home; that's the only reason why please don't be mad with me mum?"

Samantha looked at her son, "Oh darling I can never be mad with you, and we do understand so please dont worry and we would love to come round to your place and have a nice catch up with you all and of course, to have cuddles with my first grandson."

They all started to walk back to Charlotte and Andrew's house when they noticed that Paul and Gabbie were waiting outside their house, "Oh, hi, you two, what do we owe this pleasure?"

Paul looked at Charlotte, "Do you mind if we come in, please dear and explain everything inside, as its very cold out and I have a cold as well."

They all went inside, and Andrew went to make everyone a pot of tea and Patrice took everyone's coats and hung them up for them all.

While they were all waiting for the kettle to boil, Samantha had a hold of Paddy while Paul explained why they were there, "The reason we have come round today is because we took Shaky out for her walk and this lovely couple came up to us and asked us if we wanted to breed her with their dog as they wanted puppies so badly and that they couldn't find the right sort of dog for theirs."

Charlotte, Andrew, and Patrice all looked gobsmacked as they never thought about having another dog in the house but they knew if she had puppies that they wouldn't be able to give one up, "To be honest dad, we never thought about it and I mean we could have a think about it but we also have Paddy to think of as well, I mean he's not even a month old yet."

Gabbie faced her daughter with a smile on her face, "Me and your dad have been talking and we have loved having Shaky staying with us and we thought she could stay with us full time if that's okay with you Patrice, I know your parents brought her for you and we could bring the puppies up ourselves and you could visit anytime you wanted to."

Patrice went to give her gran a cuddle, "Oh that would be perfect, as it would be nice for Shaky to have another dog to play with and to look after, can we mum, dad?" Patrice asked sweetly. "And whatever pocket money I get I will give it straight to you both for Shaky?"

Gabbie gave her granddaughter a hug back, "You don't have to give us any money for her darling, don't worry, but you can come and visit her anytime you want, and you should know that by now that you don't need an appointment to come and visit us."

Andrew went to make the pot of tea for everyone as he heard the kettle whistling and Charlotte turned around to face her daughter, "Well it's up to you darling as Shaky is your dog as we did buy her for your sixteenth and we will try and support you as best we can."

Patrice went straight over to her mum and gave her a massive kiss and a hug, "Thanks mum and I think it will do Shaky some good having a pup to look after and that."

Andrew brought the tray in with a pot of tea on it and some nice biscuits that they had in the cupboard, "I have made us all a pot of tea and brought in come chocolate biscuits as well for everyone."

Not long after Samantha was holding Paddy, he started to cry and Samantha passed him back over to Charlotte as it was time for his feed, so Charlotte went upstairs to feed him and then to put him in his cot for him to have a sleep.

While Andrew was pouring everyone a cup of tea, Patrice's phone rang and its was Darren, "Hi Patrice, my mum has asked me to ask you if you fancied coming into town with us one day as she wants to meet you and we can go for something to eat as well?"

Patrice smiled down the phone, "I don't mean to be rude, but my grandparents are here can I ring you back in a little while please when they have gone?"

Darren agreed and Patrice put her phone down and she carried on having a chat with everyone and within quarter of an hour of Charlotte came downstairs, "So what have I missed then folks?"

Andrew poured Charlotte a cup of tea, "You haven't really missed much as we haven't really talked about anything."

While everyone was drinking their cups of tea, Gabbie looked outside the window, "Paul we better get going soon as I don't want to get stuck in the snow as it seems to be coming down a bit heavier now. Plus, we need to ring that couple back about letting them get Shaky pregnant also."

Samantha then turned to George, "We better get going soon as well, I feel the same way as Gabbie as I don't want to get caught up in the snow plus it's getting late now anyway."

Everyone drank up and they all left before it started snowing even faster.

Once everyone had gone, Patrice went up to her room and rang Darren back, "Hey you, sorry about before, and the answer to what you asked me is Yes, I would love to see your mum again I just hope it don't snow that bad that no one can go out and we don't get snowed in."

After an hour of Patrice being in her bedroom, Andrew shouted to her, "I have ordered pizza for tea, can you set the table, please."

Patrice came running down the stairs as she was so happy, and she set the table. After five minutes of her setting the table, the doorbell rang, and Charlotte went to collect the pizza and pays the delivery driver then she brings the pizza into the kitchen for them to sit down and have a nice chat about how they thought the day had gone.

After they had finished having tea and watched some television, they all went to bed as they were tired as they had a busy day.

CHAPTER 27

The next morning, Patrice woke up to Paddy crying as she wanted to try and have a lie in that morning as she had been getting up early for weeks. Plus, it was Saturday morning anyway which meant that was the only time she could get a lie in.

Before Patrice got up to go and have a shower to start her day as she couldn't get back to sleep now as she was wide awake, she quickly looked outside her bedroom window and she saw there was loads of snow on the ground which meant she might have been able to build a snowman with her dad if he wasn't that busy.

Patrice got ready to go into the shower as she needed to wake up a bit more, but she checked her phone before she went in the shower and she saw a text from Darren, "**Morning sexy, hope you slept well? My mum has asked me to ask you if you wanted to come shopping with us today, but we won't be getting the bus as they are not running today because of the snow but I will be driving so we could pick you up if you wanted to come with us?**"

Patrice decided to go in the shower before her mum or dad went in to get a quick shower and she had to think as well. She didn't know what her parents wanted to do; weekends are normally meant for family time.

When Patrice had finished in the shower she goes and gets dressed in her bedroom and decided to message Darren back, "**Morning, I slept good thanks and hope you slept okay as well. Am I okay to let you know in a bit please as weekends are normally family time but don't worry, I will have a word with my parents to see what they had planned for today.**"

Within a few minutes of Patrice sending that message back to Darren, he replied, "**Of course you can. Let me know as I totally understand that weekends are meant for family time, I will look forward to hearing back from you.**"

Once Patrice got downstairs, there was a visitor waiting for her in the kitchen where her parents were, Patrice stopped in her tracks and swallowed, "Ugh, yes, Terry what are you doing here? I don't want to ever see you again now will you please go and leave me alone and never get in touch with me again,"

Once Patrice said that to Terry, Charlotte and Andrew gave Patrice a stern look, "What's up darling, Terry has only come to see you. Thought you were friends, that ain't the way you talk to your friends?"

Patrice stormed off into the living room to try and get away from Terry but unfortunately Terry followed her into the living room as he wanted some answers from her, "What have I done Patrice, I only came round to talk to you as I have noticed on Darren's socials that you have been spending a lot of time with each other!"

Patrice shouted to Terry, "YOU KNOW WHAT YOU HAVE DONE! NOW, GET OUT OF MY HOUSE AND NEVER CONTACT ME AGAIN."

Terry went and left Patrice alone then her parents come into the living room as they wanted answers, "Oh darling, what has Terry done that has upset you as the other week you two couldn't keep your hands of each other and now you're arguing, and you don't want to see him?"

Patrice looked at her parents with tears coming down her face, "Please leave it. I don't want to talk about it, I am okay, don't worry, please."

Charlotte and Andrew went back into the kitchen and left Patrice to calm down, then Patrice got straight onto her phone and rang Darren, "Hey, you busy? I need to get out as Terry has just come over and we ended up having a massive argument and my parents heard it and I can't be at home at the moment."

Darren didn't know what to say as he thought weekends were for Patrice spending time with her family, "Sure I will be at yours in ten minutes or so, I will just drop my mum back off at home and we can go for a drive if you want to."

Patrice smiled down the phone as she was pleased that Darren was coming to pick her up, but she went back into the kitchen and went to stand in front of her parents, "Mum, Dad, I am sorry about that. The reason why I shouted at Terry was because he was seeing someone else right after we broke up and it hurt me a lot as I really liked him, and I thought he liked me. I am just going out for a little bit with Darren if that's fine? I know weekends are for family time, but I need to clear my head hope that's okay?"

Charlotte and Andrew nodded their heads and Patrice went to get ready, "Please don't be longer than an hour as weekends is for family time and you should know this. We don't often get to spend time with each other and now Paddy is here we might not have this time together again."

Patrice agreed and went to wait outside for Darren to turn up as she couldn't stay in that house any longer. When Darren turned up, he was really mad as he thought Terry had upset her as she was crying when she got in the car, "What did he do to you Patrice if he hurt you or anything I will kill him."

Patrice lent into Darren and gave him a kiss and a hug, "That's just the point he didn't even know he upset me when he got with that other girl, and we broke up; as I was really into him. Can we just go for a drive please as I can't be out long as my parents want to spend some time with me?"

Darren kissed Patrice back and they went for a drive, and they went to sit by the park, and they were talking for ages in the car since it was still snowing as they didn't want to go and sit in the park as it was so cold.

After them talking for a few hours, Darren drove Patrice back home, but when she got back in, she noticed that Terry was back again and she was not incredibly happy, "WHAT IN THE HELL ARE YOU DOING HERE AGAIN I THOUGHT I TOLD YOU TO STAY AWAY."

Charlotte took Patrice to one side, "Darling, I invited him back as I thought it was rude of you saying them things to him and we wanted to hear his side of things."

Patrice agreed with her mum and they both headed back into the kitchen to hear what Terry had to say, "I only went with someone else as I was hearing loads of things about you which I didn't like and I know I shouldn't have ended it with you without hearing your side of the story and that's why I came round today so we could have a chat and to warn you about Darren as he is not the man you think he is. Don't forget I have known him longer than what you have, and I know him a lot better,"

Patrice faced Terry, "Fine, let's hear your side of things then as I am all ears."

Andrew made a cup of tea for everyone as he could tell Patrice was shaking as she was cold, then Terry started off by saying, "Right I am sorry for how things turned out and I should have never dumped you as you're the only person who I think about every day, and I miss you so much. I hope you have it in your heart to forgive me?"

Patrice looked at her parents, then they both went into another room to give them some space to have a chat, "Don't worry sweetheart, you sort this out with Terry and me and your dad will go and get some fresh air and take Paddy with us, so you don't get disturbed."

Patrice smiled at her parents and then Terry and Patrice went into the living room where it was comfy to sit and then she could put the open fire on.

Once her parents had left, Patrice then turned to Terry, "I am grateful that you came and apologised to me. If we are being honest with each other, I can't stop thinking about you either and I keep looking on your socials to see what you are doing. But the thing I don't understand is why you are so against Darren for and what has he done?"

Terry then looked at Patrice with a sort of thank you smile, "I got this phone call today, from someone who we both knew, and she told me that she had a call from the cops today as Darren worked for a church a few months ago helping young people overcome their fears and for people who got raped and that."

While Terry was talking Patrice started to cry as she didn't really want to know what came next, but Terry carried on "Anyway this girl who I can't mention her name for legal reasons said, when Darren was at her house, he tried it on with her and even took her to a delightful hotel which was by the nature reserve and even booked them a nice romantic room and he paid for everything. But when they got to the room, he tried to force himself upon her even though she said NO but he carried on anyway and even pushed her onto the bed and started to drag her pants down."

Patrice looked at Terry, "Yeah, he took me to the hotel, but he never tried it on with me, unless it was because I was awake, and I knew what was going on."

Terry started to get a red face at this point, "I bet you any money if you were out of it, he would have done the same to you. Anyway, the next morning they went for a walk round the nature reserve and while they were walking Darren kept on trying it on with her repeatedly and even suggest that they try having sex in the bushes then no one would see them having sex."

Patrice shouted at Terry, "WHAT HAPPENED NEXT? YOU CAN"T JUST TELL ME HALF A STORY?"

Terry looked at Patrice, "Calm down I am just about to get to the next bit, but I was wondering if I could have a glass of water, please, as my mouth is a bit dry."

Patrice went to get them both a glass of water each then Terry carried on telling her what happened. "The next thing she knew they were heading back to his car as she had to go back home, and he asked her to marry him, and she said yes even though they only knew each other for a brief period of time. Anyway, when they were in his car, he tried to have his way with her again. He even got on top of her and then he got really rough, forcing himself upon her in his car. Even though she said no whilst trying to fight him off of her a handful of times, she then said he even put his hand over her mouth so she couldn't scream."

Patrice blurted out "OH MY GOD, IS SHE OK?" Patrice looked erratic and murmured more to herself than to Terry, "And he asked me to marry him as well and stupid me said YES."

Terry looked at Patrice with a sorry face, "You better call it off with him before you get too serious as I don't want you to get hurt or something even worse."

Patrice got her phone out straight away and sent Darren a text, "**HI, Darren I have been thinking about** what happened the other day, when you asked me to marry you, but I am sorry I can't marry you anymore as something has come up. Please don't contact me again and I am going to block you from everything. DON'T EVEN COME ROUND TO MY HOUSE."

Terry looked at Patrice, "If he comes round here again, just ring me straight away as I have a number to ring if he causes any trouble in this neck of the woods and then the police will be straight onto him and arrest him."

While Patrice was listening to what Terry had to say, she went straight onto her socials and blocked Darren from everything even from him trying to message her or even to ring her.

Patrice looked over at Terry, "Thanks for letting me know everything and I am sorry I shouted at you, but I am still a bit confused on something though and wondered if you could answer it for me, please?"

Terry nodded his head, yes sure what you puzzled about? "Are you still with your girlfriend now? As I am still madly in love with you, and I would love to give us another go if you're not seeing anyone?"

Terry smiled at Patrice, "No I am not seeing anyone and that's another reason why I came round to let you know about Darren as I can't stop thinking about you either and I wondered if you would give me another chance, please?"

Patrice went to sit next to Terry as she was sat on the chair next to him while he was sat on the sofa, "Yes I would love to give us another chance but only if you're sure you're not seeing that other woman?"

While they were both hugging each other, Charlotte and Andrew came through the door, "I take it you have both made up with each other now then if you're hugging each other?"

Patrice turned to face her parents, "Yes, both correct we have made up and Darren is ancient history and me and Terry are back together, but do me a favour please you two, if Darren comes round here asking for me don't tell him anything about where I am or anything please,"

They both faced Patrice with a puzzled look on their faces and then Terry said, "Mr and Mrs Umar, if Darren does turn up here, please ring me straight away but we can't explain why, or anything so please don't ask any question and please just trust me on this one."

Charlotte and Andrew both agreed and then Terry left them all alone to have some family time.

It was getting late, and Patrice had enough for one day as she was still a bit upset because of what she heard from Terry today as she even said yes, to Darren; and she was overwhelmed in a way that she knew all this before they got married or progressed in their relationship. "Mum dad, I am going to go to my bedroom if you don't mind as I am a bit tired as I have had a bad day today once Terry told me everything about Darren as I thought I could trust Darren but obviously I can't anymore."

Charlotte and Andrew both turned to face their daughter, "Okay night darling sleep well and don't forget don't let the bed bugs bite and we both love you loads."

Patrice faced her parents again before she walked upstairs, "Love you both too, and hope you both sleep well as well and hope we can all go out somewhere tomorrow as I would love to go ice-skating one day as I have never been."

Charlotte looked at Andrew when Patrice went up to bed, "I think we should do that tomorrow and I will ask your mum if she would like to babysit then we can all have a go what do you think?"

Andrew smiled at Charlotte, "What a great idea I will message my mum now if you want to go online and book somewhere for us to go."

When Andrew got his phone out to text his mum, he realised that his mobile was dead so he quickly put it on charge in the bedroom and then sent his mum a text, "**Hi mum, sorry to text you this late, but me and Charlotte was wondering if you and George are busy tomorrow as we want to take Patrice ice skating and we were wondering if you wanted to look after Paddy for us?**"

Andrew was shocked that he had a text back straight away from his mum as he thought she would be asleep, "**Evening darling we are awake anyway so you didn't wake us, that would be brilliant as we have nothing planned and we were thinking of coming to see you all tomorrow anyway but since you want to take Patrice ice-skating, we would love to look after Paddy for you but can we do it at yours please as we don't have any stuff here for him.**"

Andrew went to Charlotte who was just checking everything downstairs to make sure everywhere was secure and to check that the alarm is set, "Guess what, sexy? My mum has agreed to have Paddy tomorrow for us, but she said she would have to have him at ours as she don't have anything at hers for him but that's ok ain't it darling?"

Charlotte nodded her head before saying, "Or...maybe they want to come with us?" Andrew went straight back upstairs and replied to his mum,

"**Hi mum I have just had a word with Charlotte about you coming here tomorrow to look after Paddy and she said that's fine for you to look after him at ours, but then she suggested why don't you come with us?**"

Andrew didn't expect a reply as it was late, so Andrew got into bed and waited for Charlotte to come to bed so they could have a nice cuddle before they went to sleep.

CHAPTER 28

The next morning, Andrew and Charlotte decided to wake up early to sort everything out before Patrice got up as they wanted to surprise her, Andrew then checked his phone to see if his mum had replied to him and she had, "**Morning darling, that would be great as I would love to see you all ice-skating and it will also give me and George some fresh air as well as we hate staying in then me and George will buy us all some dinner. What time do you want us at yours?**"

Andrew looked at his watch, and once Charlotte came back from the shower, he looked at her and said, "My mum has said, she would love to come with us, and she would buy us all some dinner afterwards as well and she also asked what time to be here. What do you think?"

Charlotte got dressed while she had a think, and while Andrew was holding Paddy, "Why don't you go and pick your mum up now ready for when Patrice is awake then we can all go to the ice rank then. However, I was thinking why don't we blindfold Patrice so she doesn't know where we are going?"

Andrew looked at Charlotte in a shocked sort of way, "What a great idea as I love surprising our daughter."

Andrew got straight back onto his phone so he could text his mum back, **"Hi mum, I have just had a word with Charlotte, and I can come and pick you both up in an hour or so if that's good and bring you back here?"**

Charlotte decided to do a quick clean through while Paddy and Patrice were still fast asleep, "Okay, darling I am going to leave now, won't be long depending on the traffic." "It's okay, just make sure you have your keys as I am going to do a quick clean whilst the kids are asleep."

Andrew nodded and he locked the door behind him while Charlotte went to get the Hoover, but just as she was just about to unravel the lead and plug it in Paddy woke up and started to cry. Charlotte left the vacuum cleaner unplugged for now and went upstairs, she didn't want to leave Paddy crying in case it woke Patrice up.

After an hour of Andrew picking his mum and stepdad up, he came back home and made everyone a cup of tea before they all set off. However, he noticed that Patrice was still in bed, "Patrice, darling it's time to get up now as it's ten, come on sleepy head, big day planned, plus your nanna and granddad are here to see you."

Patrice got up as quickly as she could as she loved seeing her grandparents, "Morning nanna and granddad hope your both well it's nice to see you again."

Charlotte came downstairs with Paddy in her arms, "Morning Sam and George hope your both okay, and thank you so much for coming today we appreciate it. Hope Andrew has made you both a cup of tea as it looks freezing outside."

Sam and George both nodded their heads then Patrice went back upstairs to get ready. Charlotte then quietly explained the plan to them both as she didn't want Patrice knowing what they were planning to do.

When Patrice came back down all dressed, she noticed that everyone had their coats on, "Where are we going...oooh it ice skating?"

Andrew looked at his daughter with a sad face, "I am sorry darling we are not going today as we can't afford to do it now Paddy is here, we are going to someplace else which is a surprise. So can you put this blindfold on please when you get in the car."

Patrice didn't know what to think, but she did as she was told anyway. "Okay dad I will do."

Once everyone was in the car, they all set off to go to the mystery location that they all knew apart from Patrice as it was going to be a pleasant surprise for her.

When they got to the ice rank, and they had parked up, Andrew took off the blind fold on Patrice and they all smiled at her, "SURPRISE hope you like the surprise darling?"

Patrice went straight to her parents and gave them both a massive hug, "I sort of knew we was coming here as I know when you are both lying to me." Patrice laughed and pulled a clever face at them. Charlotte looked at Andrew, "How do you know we were lying, we never lie, never at all."

Patrice started to laugh at her parents, "Because I heard you whispering to each other when I went upstairs as I stood at the top of the stairs to see if you would book anything like this and you have, even though dad said we couldn't afford anything like this because of Paddy."

Andrew turned to face his daughter, "Right, darling you have us, but we didn't lie at all, we just bent the truth a bit, as we can't afford this really, but you have been through so much, we wanted to treat you."

Patrice was ever so happy anyway, "Nanna and Granddad, are you ice-skating with us as well?"

Sam looked shocked, "I can't ice-skate Patrice, but if you want me to, I will have a go, but, me and your granddad might have to take it in turns to look after Paddy though as that's the only reason why we have come so you can ice-skate with your parents."

Patrice ran straight over to the kiosk to pay as she was so excited, "COME ON NANNA LETS HAVE A GO."

Sam didn't know what to do, but she knew that she would never let her granddaughter down for nothing, "Okay, sweetheart I will be straight over."

While Patrice was waiting for her nanna to come and join her, Patrice got them a pair of skates each as that would save time and they can then go straight onto the ice rink.

Sam joined Patrice after ten minutes of trying her best to get out of it, but she saw her granddaughter's face light up when she had the skates in her hand, "I am on my way darling."

While Sam was on her way to meet with Patrice, Andrew shouted, "WAIT FOR ME, I might come and join you both if that's okay, if one of you falls over then you will need a big strong man to pick you up."

Both Sam and Patrice laughed, "yeah okay then strong man you can join us."

Patrice was having a whale of a time on the rink with her nanna and her dad who is her rock, "Thanks for this dad, I am having a right laugh especially when you keep falling over and I have to keep helping you up."

Andrew looked at Patrice, "It was your mum's idea as well darling, so you really need to thank her."

Patrice skated over to where her mum and granddad were and we can't forget about little Paddy, "Hi mum, how do you think I am doing on the ice, I can't believe that dad has fallen overloads of times when he thought either me or nanna would fall over but we showed him didn't we mum? I think you and dad need to swap over now and you come on the ice and try and show dad up, as I am sure you told me years ago that you always used to come skating at the weekends with your mates?"

Charlotte went all read faced, "Oh I can't remember telling you that, but you have a good memory of the past anyway. To tell you the truth darling I think your dad's having too much fun on the ice and I don't want to spoil that for him, and I have

Paddy to look after even though your nanna and granddad came to help as well."

Andrew saw Patrice talking to her mum, so he skated towards them, but of course he was holding onto the sides as he didn't want to fall over again as he was already in pain from the previous times he fell over on the ice. "Charlotte, I think it's your turn to come on the ice rink now and show us how it's done since you used to ice skate when you were younger."

Charlotte gave Andrew a nasty look, "Oh fine then Andy you want to play like that then do you and you want me to show you how its properly done?"

Andrew blew Charlotte a kiss and then he went to sit down to take his skates off and to go and fetch Charlotte some as it was her turn to go on the rink now. "Here you go darling, I have gone to fetch you some ice skates so you can have a go and show you how it's properly done. To be honest I think my mum has had enough as she has not moved from the side of the rink for ages now and I am worried about her."

While Charlotte was getting her skates on, Andrew went over to where his mum was standing, "Hold onto my arm, mum, and I will get you back to where it's safe. I will have a word with Patrice for getting you up on the rink when you didn't really want to go on."

Sam turned and grabbed hold of her son's hand, "Please don't have a go at Patrice, because if I minded, I wouldn't have gone on the rink with her, and you know I will do anything for her as she's my only granddaughter."

Andrew helped his mum to where the seats were, "Here you go mum, have a sit down for a bit, and don't worry I won't say anything to Patrice as I know you will do anything for her. Do you think you will be coming back on later?"

Sam looked shocked at her son, "I don't know yet son, and thinking about it, I think George should have a go as well, even though we are here to look after Paddy, but now I am back I think George should have a go on the ice."

George looked at Sam, "I don't know darling, even though it looks like fun, I don't have any skates?"

Andrew looked at George in a puzzled sort of way, "Let me guess you're a size 9, aren't you?

George looked puzzled back at Andrew, "How did you guess?"

Andrew sat down on the seat next to George and he passed him his skates for him to have a quick go on the ice while Andrew sat down with his mum looking after Paddy and they had a lovely chat while everyone else was having so much fun on the ice rink.

After an hour of Patrice, Charlotte and George having a wonderful time on the ice rink, they all came back to where the others were sitting, and Patrice looked at her dad with a huge smile on her face, "I have had a great time, but if I am being honest, I am getting a bit hungry now can we all go for something to eat please?"

Charlotte looked at Andrew, "Yes I think that's a great idea, as I think little man also needs a nappy change as he stinks, and I am surprised neither of you men could smell him."

Andrew laughed at Charlotte, "To be honest dear, I was just about to go and change him but then Patrice came over and said she was hungry why don't we all go to the restaurant here for some food as I think they do a lovely menu a I had a quick look when I went to the toilet"

Charlotte, Patrice, and George all came off the ice rink and they all took their skates off and when they went to return them, they noticed that the restaurant was shut for maintenance, "Andy, I thought you said that the restaurant was open, it has a huge sign on the door saying its shut for maintenance?"

Andrew looked at Charlotte, "When I walked past it the lights were on, and I didn't actually look at the front door did I or otherwise I would have known it was shut."

Patrice looked at everyone, "Why don't we just go for a Mcdonalds as that's round the corner and I am starting to smell Paddy now as he really needs a nappy change."

Everyone agreed and they all went around the corner from the ice rink and went into Mcdonalds and Patrice went to get a table for them all as she knew that her parents would know what she wanted as she always has the same thing all the time.

After they all had their food, they all went back to Andrew's and Charlotte's house for a nice hot chocolate. It was getting rather late when Sam and George looked at their watches and Sam said to Andrew, "Thank you for a lovely day we have enjoyed it son, but it's getting late now we better get going."

Andrew looked at his wife in a sorry sort of way, "Darling can I have a quick word with you in the kitchen please?"

Charlotte nodded and they both went into the kitchen, "If you're going to ask me what I think you're going to ask me then I think it's a great idea that your mum and George stay for the night as we have plenty of room here."

Andrew smiled at his wife then they both went back into the living room, "Mum, me and Charlotte have just had a quick chat with each other, and because it's late; why don't you both stay here for tonight as we have plenty of room here."

Sam smiled back at her son, "Oh that would be great thanks son, and just to show you both how grateful we are, why don't you both go down to the pub and spend some quality time with each other as we can look after Paddy for you as I know Patrice won't need looking after as she's a big girl now?"

Charlotte was so pleased that Sam had suggested that "Only if you're sure Sam as I don't want to put you out and I was only thinking the other day that me and Andy won't get much time to spend with each other now that Paddy is here and don't get me wrong, I wouldn't change him for the world as I love him to pieces."

Andrew gave his mum the biggest hug that he had ever given her, "Are you sure mum as Paddy can be a bit of a handful, I tell you what we will just be an hour and I will take Paddy upstairs and put him down for his sleep if you could just listen out for him that would be perfect thanks."

Charlotte and Andy went to go and get changed into something nice and then they headed out to the local pub which was only round the corner from where they live. "We will just be an hour tops and Patrice be good for your nanna and granddad, please hunny."

Patrice smiled at her parents, "I am always good you should know that, and I am going to go up to my room now as I have a book, I need to finish reading which is quite good so I will say night to you all now."

Charlotte and Andy went to give Paddy a good night kiss and they also gave Patrice a kiss as well then, they headed out of the door to go for a quick pint on their own.

CHAPTER 29

The next morning, Sam couldn't sleep as she kept on having nightmares about her ex-husband, so she decided to get up and make everyone some fresh toast for breakfast with either a glass of pure orange or a cup of tea or coffee.

After an hour of Sam making breakfast, Andrew woke up in a shock as he could hear loads of banging around and he thought it might have been Darren coming back to scare them all, so he headed downstairs very quietly with a baseball bat in his hand ready to hurt the little twit, "Oh it's you mum, you scared me as I thought we had some burglars, what are you doing up so early?"

Sam turned around to face her son, "I am sorry if I was making too much of a noise, I tried to be quiet, but I don't know where anything is in the kitchen. Now you're up do you fancy a cuppa?"

Andrew looked to see what time it was, and it was only eight, "Can I have a cup of tea please mum, but I will just go and jump in the shower first as I smell, and I have a bit of a headache as well."

Sam nodded and carried on making breakfast while Andrew went back upstairs to get ready for his shower and to just let Charlotte know that his mum was making breakfast.

Paddy was still asleep at this point, and Andrew woke Charlotte up gently, "Morning sweetheart, I have just had a crazy idea, you know while Paddy is still asleep and to save water, do you fancy jumping in the shower with me while George and Patrice are still asleep, as my mum is making breakfast and don't forget we have En-suite in our bedroom as well for emergencies that we can sneak into so my mum won't know either?"

Charlotte leant over to see what Paddy was doing and she noticed that he was still fast asleep, "Okay then why not, as I enjoyed our date night last night and if I am being honest, I didn't want it to end as we had such a laugh and it was like when we first met, all those years ago."

After they had their shower, they went downstairs for some breakfast that Sam had made, "Morning Sam how are you feeling this morning? Hope you and George slept well?"

Sam turned around from cooking some food on the stove, "I slept...okay, I guess thanks how about you two after your date night? I think George is still asleep as I have not heard any movements upstairs apart from you two coming down."

While they were all talking, George and Patrice came downstairs, "Morning everyone hope you're all, good?"

After everyone had a quick chat to see how they all slept, Sam served up breakfast for them all, "I have made everyone eggy bread, hope you all like this as I know that Andrew couldn't get enough of this when he was younger as he always had this at weekends."

Andrew looked at his mum with a huge smile on his face, "I can't believe that you remember I loved this when I was younger as I have missed having this as no one made it like you did."

Once everyone had breakfast, George and Sam got ready and said their goodbyes to everyone and they set off back home. But before they left Andrew and Charlotte had something to say to them both, "We appreciate everything you have done for us today and last night; we really do appreciate it as we couldn't have done it without you two looking after Paddy; don't forget our door is always open for you both to come round whenever you want to see us."

Sam and George smiled at Charlotte and Andrew and gave them both a huge hug and Sam said to Andrew, "Give Patrice my love won't you please darling, as I don't know where she is as I wanted to give her a hug and some spending money but looks like I will have to give it to you. Make sure she gets this twenty please darling."

Andrew didn't look happy when his mum gave him this much money for his daughter, "Oh mum that's too much for her, why don't you swap it for a tenner instead as you can't afford that especially when you're on a pension."

Sam smiled back at her son, "Okay then darling, let's do it this way, give ten to put aside or by something nice for Paddy and the other ten, to Patrice than its fair, how's that?"

Andrew and Charlotte smiled at Sam and then they left to go home, when they had left, Charlotte looked at her husband, "I have had a great idea, why don't we all go on a camping holiday for a few days and when we get back home Patrice can then go back to school?"

Andrew went upstairs to find where his daughter was, when he got to the top step, he found her coming out of the bathroom, "You okay darling it looks like you have been crying? Nanna has given you and Paddy a tenner each and me and your mum have been talking and we were thinking we could all go on a camping trip for a couple of days what do you think?"

Patrice had always wanted to go camping with the family, "I think that is a great idea, as the last time I went camping was when I was in my homegroup with church, and we all went away for a week can you remember dad?"

Andrew looked shocked, "How can you remember that as you were only youngish but then again you can remember a lot about your childhood can't you?"

When Andrew had finished talking to Patrice, he went back downstairs to see what Charlotte was doing, "Hey darling, Patrice is on board with us going away for a few days camping, but then I had a thought I don't think you would love camping because of all the creepy crawlies, so why don't we all go to a cabin which is half an hour away and it also has a hot tub as well?"

Charlotte got straight onto the internet and looked up places where they could go which had a hot tub, "I have found a place nearby which is called Zoom way and that has a suitable cabin with a hot tub outside on the balcony and there is a kids play area on site as well for Paddy, shall I go ahead and book it but it's going to cost about four hundred pounds for all of us can we afford it though?"

Andrew looked at his wife with a smile on his face, "Don't you worry about money at the minute, as I will use my credit card to pay for it and I can pay it back when I get back at the end of the month."

Charlotte went ahead and booked it then she shouted up to Patrice, "Darling, can you come down here for a minute please as we have something to tell you."

Patrice came running albeit carefully down the stairs as she was so excited about going away even if it was for a couple of days, "Yes mum I am here, I am not in trouble, am I? If it's to do with going away that's a great idea as Dad was telling me that we are going camping, and I can't wait."

Andrew looked so sad at his daughter, "I am sorry darling, I got it wrong we are not going camping, but we are going somewhere else which is a lot better because then we won't have to deal with your mum screaming all the time cause of the spiders and all of the creepy crawlies." He laughed whilst rubbing Charlotte's shoulder affectionately

Patrice started to look puzzled as her dad promised her, they were going camping, "If we are not going camping then where are we going?"

Charlotte picked up her laptop and took it over to where Patrice was standing. "Here is the place and it's called Zoom way and it's only an hour's drive away from us and it won't be too far in case we have forgotten anything then we can come back. What do you say sweetheart you fancy it?"

Patrice jumped for joy as she had heard everyone in her school go on about this place when she was in school, and they were all saying it's good for the money. "I can't wait, as when I was at school, everyone was on about it as they had been there with their parents and even went there with their other half's so yer I can't wait. But when are we going?"

Charlotte looked at time on her watch, "Well we can go later today, but you will need to go and pack now as I think your dad is packing for me and him and of course, Paddy, while I get some bits sorted in the living room. Oh, don't forget your swimming costume as there is a hot tub there as well."

Patrice went running back upstairs and she started packing loads of things and throwing them in her bag, while she was packing her bag, her phone rang, "Hey, Terry are you okay? I can't talk for long as I am just packing as we are going away for a few days to Zoom way which is an hour's drive away from ours."

Terry sounded shocked as he was so jealous as he had no one to take there, but he never knew anyone. "Oh, wow I have always wanted to go there as I have heard loads of nice things about it, and I have heard also that you can take your own alcohol as well."

Patrice sounded shock with what Terry had just said, "Oh can you? Bet my parents didn't even know that unless my mum had read that bit but not said anything because of my dad who loves a drink when he's off work. Wish you could come as well but don't worry I will send you loads of pictures of me and the porta-cabin when we get there."

Once Patrice had got off the phone with Terry, she carried on packing but because she didn't know what to pack, she just packed a load of clothes, "Hey mum, did you know you could take your own alcohol with us, and would that mean I can have a drink as well; as you sometimes let me drink at home but only on special occasions?"

Charlotte quickly checked the description of the porta-cabin again, "Oh so it does, and I suppose so since we are going away, and did I hear you on the phone with Terry saying you wish he was coming with us?"

Patrice nodded her head, "Yes you heard rightly but don't worry I can catch up with him another time as this is about family time and he understands that."

Once everyone had finished packing, Andrew took everything to the car and made sure they had enough room to sit and then after a few minutes they all set off.

On the way to Zoom way, they all played a game called "Have you ever" and when they arrived, Patrice was the first person out of the car as she was dying for the toilet, "Sorry mum I have to rush to the toilet as I am desperate and I also need to message Terry to let him know we have arrived safely but I will be straight back to help unload the car."

Once Patrice got back to the car, she realised that everything was out of the car, and they were all waiting for her to return so they could have a look around the camp site.

While they were having a look around, they spotted a nice little pub on site which served food and drink, and it was now getting near to teatime, so they went to have a look inside and had a quick look at the menu which they loved the look of, so they went to get a table and Andrew went to the bar and placed the order for them all.

While they were eating tea, Charlotte's phone stared to ring and it was her mum, "Hi mum is everything well? We have just come away for a few days to have some family time and we have come to this lovely place which is an hour away from us called Zoom way."

Gabbie didn't sound particularly good over the phone, "Oh hope you have a lovely time, as I was just ringing with some good news about Shaky, can you remember we came and told you about this couple who came and asked us to see If we wanted to breed her with their dog? Well, we went ahead and did it since Patrice said it was okay and now, she's pregnant and she is going to be having some pups."

Charlotte was ever so pleased with the news, and she passed the phone to her daughter, "Hi Gran is everything okay? How's Shaky? Is she pregnant yet?"

Gabbie couldn't get a word in edge ways, "Hi darling, yes Shaky is fine and that is why I was ringing your mum to tell her the good news, she is now carrying five pups, but we don't know the sex of them just yet as we only found out this morning that she was pregnant."

Patrice was over the moon, "Oh wow give her a big kiss from me and tell her I miss her and that I will come round soon and see her."

After Patrice put the phone down, they all carried on eating, and it was getting dark by now and they thought they better get back to the porta-cabin and get Paddy settled in for the night.

When they all got back, they all decided to get an early night as Charlotte and Andrew thought they would take a drive somewhere tomorrow as they realized there was not much to do on site.

Charlotte and Andrew gave Patrice a kiss goodnight and they went to their bedroom while Patrice went to hers and she was texting Terry for most of the night and was sending him loads of lovely pictures of the place just to make him a bit jealous. "Just thought I would send you a goodnight text and I hope you enjoyed the pictures I sent you of the porta-cabin that we are staying in. Hope you will dream of me tonight as I know I will be dreaming of you all night."

After a few minutes of Patrice sending that text, she got a reply straight back "I always dream about you every night and yes, I did like the pictures, and I wish I was with you keeping you nice and warm. Sleep well and speak tomorrow if you want to."

CHAPTER 30

The next morning, Paddy was the first person to wake up, as he was crying loud which also woke Patrice up, so she decided to get up and make her parents a cup of tea, "I have made you both a cup of tea and I have made some toasted teacakes as well for us for breakfast if you're hungry?"

Andrew came out of their bedroom, "Morning darling did you sleep well? Sorry if Paddy woke you up with him crying as I don't think he is used to sleeping in his travel cot?"

Patrice looked and smiled at her dad, "It's fine dad, don't worry as that is what babies do. Your cup of tea is on the side if you want me to go and fetch it for you? Is mum still asleep or she is feeding Paddy?"

Andrew went to fetch his cup of tea, "She is feeding Paddy at the minute, but you can go and say hi if you want to and take her a cup of tea you have made if you want?"

Patrice knocked on her parent's doors, "It's okay darling you can come in. I am just feeding Paddy but it's fine. Did you sleep well darling as I know these beds are not that comfy are they, but they are only for a few days!"

Patrice went inside and shut the bedroom door behind her and sat at the end of the bed, "I have made you a cup of tea mum, as I was awake anyway as I heard Paddy crying, but it's fine as I wanted to make us all some breakfast."

After Patrice took her mum a cup of tea in and gave her and Paddy a good morning kiss she went back into her room and put on some warmer clothes as she was so cold, she couldn't stop shivering.

Once Patrice got dressed, she went for a look around and to have a look at the gift shop but while she was looking around, she noticed that Terry was there. "Terry I was just about to text you to see how you was this morning but I don't have to now since you are here. By the way why are you here anyway?"

Terry didn't know if to tell her the truth or to lie to her, "To be honest, I was so jealous that you have come here, so I decided to come and look around to see why everyone was talking about it plus I know the owner as this is a family business and I came down to see if my brother was working as I was going to try and get your parents a discount for your stay."

Patrice looked ever so shocked as she didn't know that his family ran this, "Oh wow I didn't know your family ran this place, it's such a lovely place as well and did you find your brother?"

Terry smiled at Patrice, "Yes I found him thanks, and I managed to get you some money knocked off the price as well, and once I got off the phone to you this morning, I decided to bring my parents down for the weekend as they have both been working so hard and I wanted to treat them."

While Terry and Patrice were talking, Andrew came to fetch her, "Patrice it's time to go now as we are going out for the day today as there is not much to do here during the day and we don't want Paddy getting bored, do we?"

Patrice smiled at her dad, "Okay Dad, I won't be long, and I have just bumped into Terry and you're never going to believe this either, his family run this business, but I will let him tell you the rest as he's just nipped to the toilet."

Just about when Patrice and Andrew were about to leave the gift shop Terry shouted, "Oh no are you going now? Hello Mr Umar hope you and Mrs Umar are well and of course baby Paddy? Oh, I nearly forgot to say Mr Umar, I have managed to get you a discount for your stay here as well"

Andrew turned to face Terry, "Oh thank you Terry that was so nice of you. Are you staying here then or just come to visit your family?"

Terry smiled at Andrew, "No Sir, I have brought my parents down for the weekend as thought I would treat them seeing as they have been working so hard and they have not had a break for over a year as they are always busy working."

After Andrew had a nice little chat to Terry, they left Terry and headed back to their porta-cabin as Charlotte was waiting for them to come back so they could go out for the day. "Where have you two been as you have been gone ages when you knew I wanted us to go out for the day."

Patrice gave her mum a sorry look, "It was my fault mum, as I bumped into Terry, and he told me that his family run this business and he has managed to get us a discount, but I don't know how much yet as dad came to fetch me before I could even get a chance to ask him."

Charlotte couldn't stay mad at her daughter, "Oh don't worry sweetheart and that was very nice of him, is he staying here as well then?"

Patrice nodded to her mum then they all set off on an adventure somewhere so they could spend some quality time with each other.

While they were driving around to try and find somewhere to go, Andrew saw a sign that said, "Welcome to The Mystery Place where you don't know what will happen?"

Andrew looked at his daughter who also noticed the sign and she was smiling at it as she had always fancied doing something with a bit of a mystery, "Shall we go and see what this is about as I can see you smile Patrice?"

Patrice and Charlotte shouted, "YES LET'S GO AND SEE WHAT THIS IS LIKE."

Once Charlotte parked up the car up, she went to pay for parking for a few hours, then they headed up to the reception to see what this is all about, "Excuse me, but we were just interested to see what sort of mystery this is please as we are intrigued and wondered how much it would be for a family to go and have a go?"

The receptionist smiled at them, "I am not allowed to say much I am afraid, but I can tell you that you will enjoy it and it is a bit creepy though will the little man be, okay?"

Charlotte looked a bit worried, "How creepy is this place? As surely you can tell us what this is about because we have a little baby?"

The receptionist looked at Charlotte and thought to herself, "Okay then although I am not really allowed to say anything, but you seem like a nice family, and I don't want you to get creeped out or anything. Put it like this, is a mystery maze and you will have to be careful which way you go as things can jump out at you and scare you and you might get a bit lost as you can also walk through the maze which will take you someplace else."

Patrice was ever so excited about this, "Can we please do this you two as this sounds wicked, and I can't wait to see what happens?"

Charlotte and Andrew looked at each other then they had a little whisper to each other, "Okay we will give it a try, how much is it for a family?"

The receptionist had a look at her computer, "Well for today only we have a special offer for a family for £30 when it normally costs £40, and you won't be disappointed either as we have had loads of good reviews as well."

Andrew got his wallet out and paid the receptionist, "We better have a good time or otherwise I will be coming back to you to get our money back." He winked at the receptionist, and they laughed.

When they all got into the maze, they didn't know where to start as they found all sorts of different puzzles that they had to complete to go to the next part of the maze.

When they had completed the first quiz, they went through this mysterious bit in the maze which took them back in time to when Charlotte and Andrew were younger, they had to try and spot the difference as it was a mix from when they were young to when they were growing up.

Charlotte and Andrew were puzzled and thought they were seeing things, "This can't be right, as how would they know what we were doing when we were younger to now?"

Patrice didn't know what to think of this maze now after seeing the second puzzle, "Guys I think we should get out of here as this don't seem real as like you both just said, how would they know about your childhood to now?"

They all tried to leave this part of the maze, as they couldn't figure out why they had to try and do this bit as it was to do with Charlotte and Andrew growing up.

Charlotte tried to figure out in her head by herself why this second puzzle was to do with them. "I think we need to go back to the receptionist and go and get a refund as I don't like this maze anymore."

Patrice and Andrew agreed with her, and they tried to leave the maze but for some strange reason they kept on coming back to the second puzzle which was to do with them growing up.

When they got back to where they left Charlotte started to cry, "WHY CAN'T YOU JUST LET US LEAVE THIS STUPID MAZE AS THIS IS NOT FUN AND ITS VERY PERSONAL."

After Charlotte had shouted that, they heard a voice through an intercom, "I am sorry you have to complete the second puzzle to get out, but I can change it to a maths or general question for you but when people have got to the second puzzle they do try and complete it but then they all give up and they never leave until they give us a good review."

Charlotte looked at Andrew, "What do you think, as we did pay loads of money to come and give this a go, shall we ask for another question to do with general knowledge?"

Andrew turned round to face his daughter who was starting to cry now as she was getting scared and few things make her scared, "It's up to you two as I just want to get out of here as I am getting creeped out now and I just want to go back to the cabin."

Charlotte shouted to the voice, "WE WILL TRY A GENERAL KNOWLEDGE QUESTION BUT IF WE CAN'T DO THAT ONE THEN WE WILL JUST LEAVE YOU A GOOD REVIEW WITHOUT FINISHING THE MAZE."

The voice on the intercom replied, "Okay then, you have chosen for a general knowledge question which I will do for you now."

Everyone was so relieved that the lady changed the question for them as they all know a bit of general knowledge. Andrew read the question out "As of May 2020, who played the current Dr Who? They were all trying to think of the answer as they used to watch Doctor Who, after five minutes of them all having a think Patrice shouted, "IT'S JODIE WHITTAKER."

They were all relieved that they knew the answer and they could carry on. Charlotte faced her daughter, "Darling do you want to carry on or do you want to leave as I can tell you're upset and scared like I am. Don't worry about the money your dad will sort it somehow."

Patrice looked at her parents, "I am a bit scared and worried as this is not any ordinary maze so yes, please can we leave."

Charlotte was ever so pleased that she said that, so Charlotte shouted, "WE WANT TO LEAVE NOW SO LET US LEAVE AND DONT WORRY WE WILL STILL GIVE YOU A GOOD REVIEW."

The lady turned the microphone back on, "SINCE YOU HAVE AGREED TO GIVE US A GOOD REVIEW, I WILL LET YOU GO THIS TIME."

They all ran as fast as they could to get out of this awful maze and when they got back to the receptionist, Andrew goes up to her, "Excuse me, but can we get a refund please and don't worry we will still give you a good review."

The receptionist gave them a long hard stare, "On this occasion, yes I will give you a full refund since you have agreed to give us a good rating, but only if you promise never to return here again."

They all nodded their heads, and they ran as fast as they could back to the car and drove back to the porta-cabin.

When they arrived back to camp, Patrice got out of the car first and ran straight back to her bedroom in the cabin as she didn't want Terry seeing her afraid and crying but that was too late as Terry had already seen her running back. "Excuse me Mr and Mrs Umar, but is Patrice, okay? I just seen her running back to her cabin crying?"

Charlotte faced Terry with a sorry look in her face, "No she is not okay, as we went to this maze which was down the road as we thought it was an ordinary maze, but it wasn't as you had to answer questions to get to the next round and the second question was about when me and Andrew was younger to when we were all grown up."

Terry looked shocked as he read about the maze and read loads of good things about it, "That's strange as I was looking at that the other day and I read loads of honest reviews about it. I am so sorry to hear you had a terrible experience with this."

Andrew then spoke up while Charlotte was getting Paddy out of the car, "Yes you would have read loads of good things about it, as they make you put good reviews online so they can let you leave or if you didn't agree to it than we would have still been in the maze."

Terry slumped to the ground as he was appalled by what he just heard, "Oh I am so sorry to hear that, I will ask some of my family to see if they know anything about this for you and we will also do some digging as well as I don't want Patrice being upset well actually I don't want any of you to be upset as you're a good family."

Charlotte gave Terry a hug, "Oh thank you Terry that means so much to us, and please don't say anything to Patrice will you about this as I don't want her being upset even more."

Charlotte and Andrew went to join Patrice in the porta-cabin, and they all had some dinner and watched some films that they brought with them.

After they watched a few films, it was now getting near to teatime, so they decided to go to the pub, which was on site, as they didn't dares leave the camp site now in case anything weird happened to them.

Charlotte knocked on Patrice's door as she didn't watch any films with her parents which was odd, "Darling are you okay in there as you have not been out of your room since we have got back. It's getting near to teatime now and we were going to go to the pub on site for some tea if you are joining us, I bet Terry will be there."

Patrice opened her bedroom door, "I will just get changed and sorry I didn't come out of my room for a few hours as I was planning too but I fell asleep as that maze took all my energy from me and I just needed a rest."

Charlotte gave her daughter a massive hug, "Don't worry about it darling, we are back here now, and we are safe. We will wait for you to get ready then we will all go over to the Wombats pub for something to eat and I think there is also some entertainment which might be fun."

Patrice went to go and get changed as it only took her a few minutes then they all headed over to the pub as they were all starving by now.

Once they all ordered what they wanted to eat, they went to find a table which was near the stage so they could see the entertainment that was on.

While they were all waiting, Terry came over to Patrice, "Hey how are you enjoying your stay in the porta-cabins? Have you been in the hot tub yet? As I have heard it's nice and relaxing, but I have never tried them yet myself."

Patrice turned to face Terry, "I am okay I guess thanks, and no I have not tried the hot tub yet, but I want too but I don't want everyone seeing me in there as I don't have a nice body, as I am fat."

Terry could not believe what he just heard, "You are not fat so please don't think like that."

Patrice smiled back at him, "You're so kind Terry, and thoughtful and I am glad we are back in touch with each other."

While they were talking Patrice's phone buzzed as she got a text from an unknown number, "**I see you had fun at the maze today and that you and your mother got scared and that you wanted out, but you could only leave if you gave them an honest review. I SEE EVERYTHING YOU DO PATRICE YOU CAN'T HIDE FROM ME.**"

Patrice slammed her phone down on the table after she read that awful text, Charlotte quickly turned around to face her daughter, "Darling what's the matter, you never slam your phone down like that unless you have read something you don't like or you're mad?"

Patrice showed her mum the text that she just received, "Oh Patrice why didn't you just tell me about this awful text without slamming your phone down because you might have ended up breaking your phone and we can't afford to buy you a new one."

Patrice didn't care about her phone at this point she was just wondering who sent her that awful message, when she checked her phone again, she noticed that she had another text, **"You can't go around slamming your phone as then how would I be able to contact you Miss Umar, and I see you're with your new boyfriend a well."**

After Patrice had read that second message, she got up out of her chair and left the restaurant as she couldn't take it anymore and Terry noticed her running out, so he went over to where Charlotte and Andrew were sitting, "Is Patrice okay as I have just seen her running out of the restaurant crying her eyes out again?"

Andrew looked at Terry, "She had this weird text on her phone from an unknown number saying that they knew that we went to the maze and that they saw her with you. Can you go and check to see if she's okay please, I don't think she will talk to us?"

Terry nodded and he went to find where Patrice went and the first place, he looked was at the porta-cabin, "Patrice are you in here as me and your parents are worried about you and they also told me about the texts you have had as well."

Patrice came out of her room while she was drying her eyes, "What else did my parents tell you? Bet they think I am being daft and stupid?"

Terry went over to give her a huge hug, "No don't be daft. They don't think you're being daft or stupid. If I got them sort of texts, I would have done the same as you, but have you thought about changing your number so they can't get hold of you again?

Patrice gave Terry a hug back, "But won't they charge me for changing my number? And I am fairly sure I know who it might be as it's a mutual friend of ours?"

While Terry and Patrice were talking, her parents come back as they had enough of being in the pub as it was not the same without their daughter, "How are you feeling now darling now that Terry is here protecting you?"

Patrice smiled at her parents, "I am starting to feel a bit better now that I am not alone, and I don't know if to be mad with you both for telling Terry or be pleased that you told him. I just want to know who sent these texts."

Everyone looked at Patrice with a sorry look on their faces, "We know you want to find out, but who knows we have come here as you didn't post anything on your socials did you?"

Patrice just stared at her parents, "No, why would I post that we were coming here for? It's no one's business where we go as a family, and I am so pleased that you're here Terry as I couldn't have figured out who it might be without you being here, so thank you so much and I am also sorry for slamming my phone down as well."

Terry smiled at Patrice, "You did the figuring out yourself saying it might be a mutual friend of ours, but I would definitely do what I suggested and change your number with your phone provider."

Patrice nodded as she agreed with what he had suggested, "I am going to change my number don't you worry about that. Them texts are doing my nut in as I think my phone just buzzed as its on charge."

Patrice went back into her bedroom to check her phone and when she checked it she had another text from an unknown number, "**I see that you have told lover boy about these texts I am sending you which is not clever at all as you won't be getting away with this Patrice and how you treated me I am watching your every move and I can hear everything you are saying so you better not say another word to anyone."**

After Patrice had read that message, she turned her phone off and took the sim card out, "I had another one of them texts, I really need to get a new phone with a new sim as I have just thrown mine away as this is creeping me out now."

Charlotte started to cry at this point, as she didn't like to see her daughter this upset or scared, "Right okay darling, we can go and find a phone shop and we will get you a brand-new phone and don't worry about throwing your sim away as I think that was the best idea you had."

After Charlotte had said that, Terry suggested to them, "I will go and have a look around the camp site to see if I can see anyone who is acting suspicious or anything and I will let you know when I get back. and I will also do some digging as well to see if it is this bloke is who we think it might be don't worry Patrice we will get to the bottom of this."

Charlotte grabbed the car keys from her husband, and they set off to find a phone shop nearby, "Darling you know while I am taking our daughter to get a new phone would you mind looking after Paddy for me, please as we should only be gone for an hour or so, but I will keep you up to date."

Andrew nodded as it went without saying, then Charlotte and Patrice headed off to find a phone shop. Luckily, they managed to find one half an hour away from the camp site, so they both got out of the car and went to have a look inside.

While they were looking, a shop assistant came over to them, "Good afternoon, hope you're both doing okay on this horrible day, is there anything I can help you with today?"

Charlotte smiled at the assistant, "We are just looking around at the minute but thank you as I don't know what sort of phone my daughter is after. We will come and get you once we know what sort of phone she wants if that's okay?"

Charlotte went over to where her daughter was standing and having a look at the new iPhones that are out, "Oh mum this is the up-to-date version of my iPhone as it's the iPhone 14 and mine was the 13 and it's also got better graphics as well."

Charlotte looked at the price and was shocked to see how much it was then she looked at how much it would be on contract and that would work out better if she had a contract phone.

Charlotte looked gobsmacked at the price of this phone, "Oh darling it is a bit too much for me to pay out right, but if we strike up a deal then I can afford to buy it for you on contract but every bit of pocket money you get you will have to help to pay towards this as it will cost a lot more to buy it out right so we will have to get it you on pay monthly."

Patrice smiled at her mum, "Of course I will help pay towards this as I am old enough to have a contract now... well, I hope, can I have it in the purple please mum?"

Charlotte went over to the sales assistant, "Excuse me can we get this iPhone 14 please on contract in the purple please?"

The sales assistant checked on the system to see if they had the colour that Patrice wanted, "You're in luck, it's the last one in stock I will just go and fetch it for you now ma'am."

Patrice gave her mum a massive smile and then she had a look in her purse to see if she still had some of her pocket money from her nanna and granddad that she could give to her mum. "Here is my first bit of pocket money I can give you, I am sorry it is not much though."

Charlotte smiled at her daughter, "Don't be daft darling, I was only joking as I need to make sure you're okay and when you get a part time job then you can start paying for your phone is that a deal?"

Patrice was over the moon that she got the latest model, "Of course mum and thank you so much I do appreciate this."

Once the sales assistant came back out, he said, "Right I just need to take some details from you please, and while we are inputting the details, I will also set this up for you and see if we can get you some good deals as well as some of our phones come with a games console."

Charlotte got her credit card out and proof of ID for the sales assistant, "I have just checked on the system and it says you can get a PS4 as well on this deal as its £40 a month but it will need £99 upfront cost if that is okay with you ma'am?"

Charlotte looked at her daughter who looked well pleased with this phone, "Okay then we will go ahead and get this please as it seems like a right bargain if we are getting a PS4 as well with it."

It only took the assistant half an hour to sort all of this out for them, "Right you're all done, and I hope you're happy with your product as I have put the sim in and I have turned it on for you as well but when you get back home, it will need a good charge before you properly use it."

Charlotte nodded and then they both left the shop and headed back to the camp site. When they got back, Terry was waiting for them to return, "I don't have any news for you just yet, but I have messaged Darren to see where he is and just said that I wanted a word with him if he weren't busy and if he wanted to meet up."

Patrice smiled at him, "Thank you again for trying to help me, once I have given my new phone a good charge, I will let you know my number as I don't know what it is just yet."

Terry nodded his head and before he left Patrice and her family, he was now starting to get these weird texts which said, "Hi Terry, I know you don't know me as this is an unknown number, but can I ask you a favour please and can you let your little girlfriend know that her changing her number won't stop me from messaging her or even getting in touch with her."

Terry couldn't believe that he was starting to get these weird messages now from the unknown number, "Just before I go, I thought I better warn you that whoever it is who was sending you them messages now knows that you have a new number as they have just text me saying that they won't stop texting you as they will find out your new number and they will contact you shortly."

Patrice was not going to let this person bully her anymore and that she decided to ignore them, "Oh I am so sorry that you're getting these messages now think we need to get to the bottom of this right away as it's not fair on you getting these texts now."

Terry smiled at Patrice, "No don't be daft it's fine, don't worry about me as I am big and ugly enough to look after myself, just concentrate on yourself."

Patrice went over to Terry and gave him a big kiss, "Thank you so much for being there for me today and for everything and hope you didn't mind me giving you a kiss?"

Terry went all red faced, "No of course I didn't mind actually it was quite nice you giving me a kiss."

It was getting near teatime now, Charlotte looked at Terry, "I don't suppose you have any plans for your tea tonight, do you? If not, did you want to join us in the pub for something to eat and don't worry about paying this is on us for being there for our daughter today."

Terry looked at the time, I will just have to go and check with my folks if that's okay with you Mrs Umar, and I can meet you in the pub if you want and let you know?"

Charlotte smiled and then Terry went back to find his folks while Patrice and her parents started to get ready to go for their evening meal.

When they arrived at the pub, they waited to get seated by the waitress and they did not have to wait long to get a table, "Can we get a table for six please and can we have a quick look at the menu please?"

While they were looking at the menu, Terry came over to them, "Hi Mr and Mrs Umar, I have had a word with my parents, and they have said that's fine for me to join you for tea and they also said it is very nice of you to pay for me."

Charlotte smiled at him, "Me and Andrew have been talking and we thought why don't you all join us for something to eat as it would be nice to have a catch up with your folks as well."

Terry went to find his folks and then they all sat around the table enjoying each other's company and the tribute band who were singing songs from Take That.

It was getting near to ten and it was time for Paddy to get some sleep in his cot, Charlotte looked at Andrew, "Hunny if you want to stay a bit longer, I can take Paddy back to the cabin as it's well past his bedtime, but Patrice will you come back with me please as you look shattered after today's events."

Everyone was so tired by now that they all went their separate ways and Patrice gave Terry another kiss and then they said goodnight to each other, and Patrice followed her parents back to the porta-cabin while Terry and his parents went back to theirs.

CHAPTER 31

The next morning, there was a knock on the porta-cabin door, so Patrice goes to answer it, "Morning Terry how are you today? Have you had any more texts yet?"

Terry smiled at Patrice as he was so happy to see her smile after yesterday's events, "Moring Patrice I slept fine thanks, and no I have not had any more texts thank God. I was just wondering if you fancied getting some breakfast with me and my parents this morning or are you going home today?"

Patrice didn't know what to say as she was not sure what they were doing. "Let me just go and check with my parents, and save you waiting around here, I will text you after I have spoken to my parents, but can you quickly put your number into my phone please?"

Terry quickly inputted his number for Patrice and then he went back to his cabin and waited for Patrice to let him know what was happening.

Once Patrice shut the door, her dad came out of his bedroom, "Morning Darling how did you sleep last night. I have just come to make your mum a cup of coffee while she feeds Paddy; was that Terry's voice I just heard then?"

Patrice smiled at her dad, "Yes it was, as he just wanted to know if I wanted to join him and his parents for breakfast. But I said I weren't sure if we were going home today?"

Andrew looked at his daughter with a smile on his face, "Well, me and your mum have been talking about that and we are thinking of staying one more night, but we thought we would leave that decision with you."

At this point Patrice didn't know what to think as she was still a bit scared about the stalker that she had, "I don't know to be honest, I do love this place and I still haven't tried the hot tub yet, but I am simply scared being here with all of them weird texts I have been getting. But can we just stay one more night please dad as I think Terry is going home tomorrow as well."

Andrew took Charlotte her coffee, "Morning darling, I have just been having a chat with our daughter and she wanted to stay one more night if that's still fine with you as well and she also wanted to know if she could go for some breakfast with Terry and his parents this morning?"

Charlotte smiled at her husband, "That would be fantastic as I heard Pat saying that she wanted to try the hot tub and I would love to try it as well so can we stay one more night please baby as I know you paid up until today?"

Andrew went back into the lounge to make himself a cup of tea as he forgot to make himself a drink, "Pat, I have just been talking with your mum and she also wants to stay for one more night and she said she would also love to try the hot tub as well. So, I am guessing we can stay for one more night and yes you can go for some breakfast with Terry."

Patrice got her phone out of her bag and sent Terry a text, "**Hi Terry my dad has said we can stay for one more night as me and my mum want to try the hot tub out and that I can come and join you and your parents for some breakfast. I will meet you in the bar in ten minutes as I need to get changed.**"

Not long after she sent that text to Terry she got a reply, "**Okay cool we are already in the bar waiting and we have a table as well which is near the window so you will see us sitting there. See you when you get here.**"

Patrice carried on getting changed and then she headed to the bar where Terry and his parents were waiting for her, "Morning thank you so much for inviting me to join you for some breakfast my dad's just gone to pay for another night for us to stay as me and my mum want to try the hot tub out."

After they all had breakfast, Terry and Patrice went for a nice walk around the woods and they found this nice cave, which is deserted, so they decide to stay in there for a little while and have a nice chat before they headed back to their parents.

While they were in the cave, Terry couldn't keep his hands off her and Patrice was shocked, "Oh Terry, I so want to do something with you but I don't fancy doing it in this cave as people will see us if they walk past and I would feel like a right tramp doing it here."

Terry looked at Patrice, "I know what you mean but you turn me on so much as you're so sexy. I can see if there is a spare cabin we could go into for a bit if you wanted to do something as don't forget my family run this business."

Patrice smiled back at Terry, "If it's okay with you I would rather wait for a bit longer and I am not sexy at all but thanks for saying that I am."

Terry looked at Patrice with a huge smile on his face, "Of course we can wait if you want to, although we have already had sex ain't we but whatever you want."

They both started to head back to their porta-cabins so Patrice and her mum could use the hot tub, "Hi mum I am back from breakfast and me and Terry also had a nice walk after, but I thought I would come back and use the hot tub if you still fancy going in as I don't want to go in by myself and look stupid and ugly."

Charlotte looked at her daughter with a smile on her face, "Darling don't be daft, you won't look stupid and your certainly not ugly so please stop thinking like that and I will be a few minutes then we can go in together if you want?"

While they were enjoying mother/daughter time together in the hot tub Andrew stayed inside the porta-cabin as there was football on the television and he wanted to watch that in peace. "Hope you girls have fun in there while I am in here all alone with Paddy watching football."

While the women were enjoying themselves in the hot tub, Patrice had a text message with photo attachment, **"Oh wow you look so lovely in a bikini in that hot tub with your mother I just wish I was in the middle of two sexy women."**

Patrice screamed, "I CAN'T BELEIVE THIS, SOMEONE HAS JUST TAKEN A PHOTO OF US MUM- IN HERE AND SAID THAT WE

BOTH LOOK SEXY. WHAT IN GODS NAME IS HAPPENING HERE?"

After Patrice shouted that, Andrew came running out as he heard his daughter shouting, "What's the matter as I heard some shouting, but I didn't hear what was said."

Patrice showed her dad the message, "I am going to kill this son of a bitch whoever he is and he better watch out if I catch him doing this again and spying on my daughter and wife."

They both quickly got out of the hot tub as they didn't fancy staying in there anymore not after the text Patrice just had.

While they were both getting out of the tub, Terry was walking up towards them, "Is everything okay as you both look stressed and scared, is there anything I can do to help?"

Patrice went over to Terry wrapped up in a towel as she didn't want to go and get dressed just yet as she needed a hug from her boyfriend, "Oh Terry I have had another text with a picture of me and my mum in the hot tub and he said that we both looked sexy in there and that he wanted to be in the middle of us. I don't know how much more I can take now."

Terry didn't know what to do anymore as he doesn't like stalkers, "Don't worry I am going to find out who sent these messages to you and me if it's the last thing I do."

Terry took Patrice inside so she could go and get dressed, "If you want to and if it's okay with your parents, I can see if you can stay with us tonight although I know nothing will happen to you while you're with your parents."

Patrice looked at her parents, "It's up to you sweetheart, but you know we won't let anyone hurt you but again. But all we ask is if you can be back for nine as we are going to go as soon as you come back in the morning after you stay with Terry and his folks."

Patrice was in two minds in what to do even though she knew she would be safe with her parents but also, she knew she might be better off staying with Terry in case anything else happens. Terry would be better in catching this bloke then what her dad would be as Terry is a fast runner. "I love you both very much you both know that don't you? But it might be better to stay with Terry and his folks just in case we see whoever it is; as Terry is fitter and a fast runner and he would be able to catch up with the stalker."

Andrew nodded to his daughter, "Don't worry sweetheart we know what you mean, and I agree Terry would be better at catching whoever it is that is stalking you as he's younger and fitter than me."

After her parents agreed to let her stay with Terry, they both headed to his cabin and Patrice, Terry and his folks ended up having a games night.

CHAPTER 32

The next morning Patrice woke up screaming, "Patrice, are you okay, sexy, you gave me a fright with your screaming?"

Patrice started to cry frantically, "I am so sorry Terry, I had this weird dream and thought that the stalker might be watching me through your window; I know it sounds stupid, but I am sure he's watching me as I am sure I saw a shadow walking past the window."

Terry quickly got dressed as he was only wearing shorts, "I will go and have a look for that son of a bitch, and I will end this once and for all as I don't want you being frightened anymore."

When Terry got outside, he went to the reception area to try and find some of his mates to help him search for the stalker as they had a gun, and he could then shut the stalker up.

Once Terry got his mates to help him look, his mate, Duncan shouted, "Terry come here quick, I think I have found someone, I can just see a shoe sticking out and think he fell over, he is not moving."

Terry and the rest of the gang quickly ran towards Duncan, "That looks like an old mate of mine and Patrice called Darren I will just have to turn the git over to see if it is him."

Once Terry had turned him over, they found out it was not him and that it was someone else who looked like him, "No, damn, it's not our old mate which is a shame... that means he's still out there."

Terry could not believe that it was not who he thought it was, "We need to keep searching for him as I know he is here somewhere but it's just catching him in the act."

Duncan looked at Terry, "Why don't we just set up a trap for him to fall into and either you or Patrice text him and get him to meet you as bet you both still have his number don't you?"

Terry smiled at Duncan, "What a great idea bro, I will ask Patrice when I see her in a bit to send him a message as he will come and meet us if she texted him but if I text him he will run a mile."

After Terry had finished searching for the stalker with his mates, he went back to his cabin to have some breakfast with Patrice and his folks, "Patrice, I need to ask you a huge favour please as my brother Duncan suggested that if you text Darren to see if he will meet you, as I am sure he is the stalker, then we can catch him in the act or make some sort of excuse and we can see if he will stalk you then if that makes sense."

Patrice did not look to happy, "Okay... I just hope this works as I am two hundred per cent certain that it is Darren as well, but we do not have any proof do we really?"

Terry nodded and agreed with her, "That is true, but do you know anyone else who knows both of us like an ex-boyfriend or something as I cannot figure out, who it might be?"

After Terry said that Patrice got her phone out and texted Darren to see if he will meet her, **"Hi Darren, hope you are well, sorry I have not messaged you for a while I have just been busy. Anyway, just wanted to know if you were free and if you wanted to meet up and if you suggest the place and time I will be there."**

After a few minutes Patrice's phone made a ping noise, **"Hi Pat I am fine thanks and its nice hearing from you, hope you and your family are well? I would love to meet you we will have to meet somewhere no one will know us as I cannot be seen with you as I promised my folks, I would not meet up with you again. I can meet you at a pub called Umbra which is on a camp site, and it has loads of porta-cabins as well so hardly anyone will see us as they will all be busy?"**

Patrice showed Terry the message, "I still do not know about this, but anything is worth a try, and I am sure the pub on site is also called Umbra or am I wrong?"

Terry looked shocked, "Yes that is right, as there are two different pubs on site and that is one of them, and that proves that he is stalking us but why would he have an unknown number texting us?"

Patrice started to send a text back to Darren, "Ok Darren, what time shall we meet, as I can tell my parents a little lie to use their car to drive out here to meet you as I think I know where you mean. Shall we say we meet in half an hour?"

After a few seconds Patrice gets a text back, "Okay I will set off from mine now and I should hopefully be there in half an hour give or take as it depends on the traffic?"

Patrice was getting a little bit scared now, "He is just setting off now, and he said he should be here within half an hour give or take because of the traffic. You better be in the same pub as us so you can keep an eye on me as I am bricking this meeting with him after everything he put me through."

Terry smiled back at her, "Don't worry me and my family will be in the bar keeping a close eye on you and my other brother, Declan works behind the bar anyway and he can keep me posted if I have to nip out or anything; but don't worry I do not think I will have to go anywhere else."

They all headed off to the bar where Patrice was meeting Darren, and luckily, she was early. Patrice went to find a table right near the window so she can see when Darren turned up so she can give the signal that Darren has turned up.

Declan gets Patrice a nice pint of diet Pepsi to drink and he put a bit of vodka in there to calm her nerves, "This is on the house, as Terry has told me everything and I am also here to keep an eye on you, as I will have a better view then my brother would around the corner, but all I ask is if you can give me a signal like scratching your head to let me know when he's here or something then I can message Terry to let him know to get in touch with the police to come and pick him up or for them to be on standby"

Patrice nodded her head then she went to sit at the table right near the window like she said she would so she could spot when Darren was here.

After ten minutes of her waiting, Darren turned up, Patrice scratched her nose then her head, which Declan knew to be the signal, he then walked to the other end of the bar, he gave the thumbs up to his brother to ring the police, quickly darting back in eyesight of Patrice as Darren strolled into the bar and looked around.

TO BE CONTINTUED........